THE TWENTIETH TERRORIST

WAYNE E. BEYEA

THE TWENTIETH TERRORIST

iUniverse books may be ordered through booksellers or by contacting:

iUniverse
1663 Liberty Drive
Bloomington, IN 47403
www.iuniverse.com
1-800-Authors (1-800-288-4677)

ISBN: 978-1-5320-5670-3 (sc)
ISBN: 978-1-5320-5672-7 (hc)
ISBN: 978-1-5320-5671-0 (e)

Library of Congress Control Number: 2018911240

Print information available on the last page.

iUniverse rev. date: 09/21/2018

DEDICATION

To the victims of the terrorist attack that occurred on

September 11, 2001. You shall never be forgotten!

PROLOGUE

In the closing segment of "The Treasure of Valcour Island," Imam Omar Muhammed Bashoul, aka, Abdul Markesh; on 9/10/01, was committed to the Clinton County, New York, jail after being charged with Murder and Attempted Murder. As Bashoul was led from the court room he yelled out in anger, "Weston, you may gloat in victory tonight, but your victory will be short-lived. Tomorrow, Allah shall inflict his wrath upon you infidel dogs and bring America to its knees. Alihu Akbar!"

New York State Police Senior Investigator Tom Weston was relieved when the nightmare to arrest a diabolical, clever, sociopath was brought to an end. The investigation to apprehend Bashoul had been tiring and stressful. Now that Omar Bashoul was behind bars, Tom looked forward to enjoying more time with his family.

Tom attributed Bashoul's angry outburst in the court room as merely the idle threat of an egotistical psychopath. He had no way of knowing that a diabolically evil and destructive attack upon America by Al Qaeda terrorists would impact the idyllic north country of New York State and trigger a greater nightmare than the one he had just experienced.

1

Tom opened one eye and glanced at the illuminated clock on the stand beside his bed. The number displayed was 6:30. He arose, sat on the edge of the bed and muttered, "Tom Weston, why did you persist in closing out the bar." He massaged his scalp in a futile attempt to remove the throbbing in his head.

Normally, Tom carefully measured his intake of alcohol; however, putting the scumbag who murdered Stan LaPierre, and nearly murdered his brother, Jack, behind bars, was cause to celebrate. Bashoul had proven that he was intelligent, clever and likely a diabolical genius. Bashoul's agents left a trail of death and destruction in carrying out their Imam's orders, while trying to secure the treasure discovered by Stan LaPierre and Jack Weston; while Bashoul remained safely out of reach in Canada. It had taken a creative stroke of genius, the cooperation of numerous police agencies, and lots of luck, to trick the diabolical sociopath, and cause his arrest. Justice had at last prevailed and those who worked diligently on the case had cause to celebrate.

The head massage proved useless in trying to ease the throbbing. However, Tom was certain that a couple of Tylenol and the passage of time would alleviate the problem. A shave and shower would also aid the recovery process, and as he exited the shower, he felt much improved.

A half hour later, feeling much better, New York State Police

Senior Investigator Tom Weston greeted his wife in the kitchen of their comfortable lakeside residence, located on the west shore of beautiful Lake Champlain.

"Good morning Honey! Sorry, I had too much to drink and arrived home so late, but Jack is alive and we had much to celebrate."

While speaking, he reached for the coffee pot and poured a mug full of his most addictive beverage.

Liz pecked her husband of twenty-five years on the cheek and handed him the morning newspaper, saying as she did, "You and Jack are now celebrities. I know why you didn't arrive home until 3 a.m. You certainly had cause to celebrate. What can I fix you for breakfast?"

Forcing a smile, Tom replied, "My stomach is still rebelling from last night. Thanks, but I will go with a bowl of cereal and coffee."

Tom settled into his chair at the kitchen table and focused on the "Plattsburgh Press Republican." The front page headline declared, "Local Man Returns from Dead!" The accompanying article stated: "Peru resident, Jack Weston, who had his obituary reported in this paper on August 14, made a surprise appearance last evening, in Plattsburgh Town Justice court, very much alive! Weston was the surprise, star witness against Montreal resident Abdul Markesh, aka, Omar Bashoul, charged with the murder of Peru resident; decorated Marine veteran, Stanley LaPierre. State Police based at Plattsburgh, had reported to the Press-Republican that LaPierre was tortured and murdered at his residence located on Bear Swamp Road, in the Town of Peru. Police reported the motive for LaPierre's murder was an attempt to get LaPierre to reveal the whereabouts of a fortune in gold coin that LaPierre and associate Jack Weston, had recovered from Lake Champlain.

It was reported in the Press-Republican on August 2, that

diving partners Stanley LaPierre and Jack Weston discovered a trove of gold coins inside a cave beneath Valcour Island. The gold coins were identified as part of the cargo of a French ship which in 1751 departed Montreal on a voyage to the south-end of Lake Champlain. The ship's cargo consisted of chests of gold coins, meant as payment for troops stationed at Fort Carillon, which today is known as Fort Ticonderoga. Unfortunately, the ship struck a reef at the south end of Valcour Island, very near the smaller Garden Island. While the upper portion of the ship was above water, the cargo hold containing the gold was underwater. This occurred in the fall of the year when Lake Champlain was at its lowest water level. The crew could not salvage the gold, so the captain decided to leave a contingent of men on Garden Island, with provisions to sustain them, for the duration of the winter. He then proceeded to Fort Carillon in long boats, intending to return in the spring with manpower and equipment that would permit salvage of the gold. That proved to be a bad decision, for the Captain did not foresee the fact that every spring, runoff of melting snow flowing into the Lake from the Adirondack and Green Mountains caused the water level to rise significantly. When that happened, the surge of water pushed the ship off the reef and it sank to the bottom of the lake, which in that location was estimated at 250 feet. Over the course of time numerous divers have searched for the lost treasure, but it was never found. How the chests of gold coin made their way into the cave beneath Valcour Island remains a mystery. Of even greater significance, the cave where the treasure was found proved to be the home of, 'Champ,' an enigmatic amphibious creature, who lived during the age of dinosaurs. For years, boaters, and residents living along the lake shore, have reported sightings of an elusive reptilian like creature in the lake. Those sightings were given no credence and attributed to an anomaly in the lake. Until the discovery by

LaPierre and Weston, 'Champ' was considered mythical and a legend.

Investigation into the murder of LaPierre and attempted murder of Jack Weston, by the New York State Police, in conjunction with the Federal Bureau of Investigation (FBI), and Canadian authorities resulted in the arrest of Omar Bashoul, aka, Abdul Markesh, age 48, of Montreal, on the murder charge.

Montreal authorities report that Bashoul/Markesh, has been in Canada for about 6 years and is owner/operator of Abdul's Specialty Store in the city. It was also reported that Bashoul/Markesh is an Islamic Imam, with ties to the Khalil-a-bashul mosque in Montreal.

After hearing testimony from Jack Weston, at last evening's preliminary hearing, in Plattsburgh Town Justice Court, Judge Frank Morrisey, ordered commitment of Bashoul to the Clinton County jail, pending Grand Jury action.

State Police Investigator Tom Weston, Uncle of Jack Weston, headed up the investigation and informed the Press-Republican, police learned Bashoul was traveling to New York City and a police task force was waiting for him to arrive at JFK airport. Bashoul was taken into custody without incident and immediately returned to Plattsburgh.

Clinton County District Attorney Warren Racette, commended the New York State Police, FBI and Canadian police for their expertise and advised that additional criminal charges will be presented to the Grand Jury."

Placing the newspaper on the table, Tom said, "Honey, you should have been there to see the smirk disappear from Bashoul's face and look of panic set in, when Jack entered the court room. Bashoul is an evil man, and I hope when our prosecution is over, he gets the 'max.' Unfortunately, as New York no longer has a death penalty, all that can be hoped for is life behind bars. That is not sufficient justice, because Bashoul is intelligent, clever and diabolical. He will probably find some way to beat a life sentence and get released. Of course it didn't take the worthless pile of dog crap long to return to his egotistical, arrogant self. When Judge Morissey ordered him bound over without bail pending grand jury action, the asshole jumped to his feet and shouted, "'Tomorrow, Allah shall inflict his wrath upon you infidel dogs and bring America to its knees! What bullshit! If his Allah is such a powerful God, then we had best renounce our Catholic faith, buy prayer rugs and convert to his crap religion."

"Tom," Liz responded, "I wish you wouldn't use so much profanity and get so angry when describing the people you arrest; especially in the presence of our children."

"My description of Bashoul was accurate," Tom responded, "and our kids aren't here. Did they get off to school this morning without causing you any problem?"

"For the most part; Mary and Susan plan on participating in cheerleading this year, and both are straight A students. That activity shouldn't affect their grades much. Jeremy has graduated to starting linebacker on the football team and Bobby plans on playing basketball. Joe is already grumbling about what a mean person his fourth grade teacher is. They all caught the school bus on time this morning and incidentally, at breakfast, Susan mentioned that she was awake when you arrived home this morning."

Displaying a look of consternation she continued, "Tom, I hate to sound like a nag, but your work and the people you work with, get more of your time and more attention than your family. If your family came first, you would already be aware of what I just informed you of."

Tom did not respond verbally; however, the look of confusion on his face was indicative that he knew his wife was right.

Liz continued in an emotional voice that displayed worry and concern: "Tom, I love you – we love you, the kids and I – and we constantly worry about you. You have over twenty years in the state police. Don't you think it's time to slow down and spend more quality time with your nuclear family?"

Tom did not immediately respond as his mind searched for an appropriate response. To avoid answering Liz's question, he picked up the newspaper, pointed to a photo associated with the article concerning Bashoul's arrest, and said, "Honey, look at this handsome State Police officer." The photo displayed the smiling face of square jawed detective Tom Weston, and had been taken upon conclusion of the court hearing.

Liz scowled, shook her head in the negative and responded, "It doesn't do my handsome husband justice."

The paragraph accompanying the photo reported, "On June 18, Senior Investigator Tom Weston, who led the investigation to capture Stan LaPierre's killer, completed 24 years in the New York State Police, and is now eligible for retirement. Weston is a North Country native and graduated from Peru High School. Weston told the Press-Republican that those 24 years in the State Police seemed to have passed in a flash. Weston added that he loves his work and probably the primary reason is that he is a member of a family of dedicated police professionals who give their all to the law enforcement profession. The article continued, Weston, entered the state police at age 23 after having served 4 years in the United States Marine Corps. After discharge from the Marines, Weston married high school classmate Elizabeth Ewald, a Peru native, and they are the parents of five children. After serving stints as a uniform trooper and investigator in various areas of New York, Weston returned to Plattsburgh to supervise the BCI unit there. He was quick to point out that the quality and expertise of the Troopers and Investigators at Plattsburgh make his job easy and enjoyable. The Weston family resides in Cliff Haven and Tom reports that cruising Lake Champlain in his boat *Hav-n-Fun* relieves stress, and provides respite from an often demanding and stressful career."

What was not reported in the article was that participation in high school athletics and the USMC had molded Weston's 6'3" body into excellent physical condition, which despite the demanding hours at work, he strived to maintain. In addition to boating, Tom, regularly jogged, biked, swam, and lifted weights to keep in good condition. Liz was greatly appreciative that her husband, the man she loved dearly, did not smoke and appreciated exercise. The only thing that she nagged him about was getting his hair cut when his blond hair started hiding the skin on his neck and failing to keep his eyebrows trimmed.

Liz pointed to the photo and said, "You look at least ten years older than you are. The photo doesn't do justice to your blue eyes and handsome square jaw. And, your wavy blonde hair appears grey in the picture."

His reply was preceded by a chuckle, "Honey, unfortunately, the pressure and stress of the investigation to apprehend Bashoul, aged me ten years. You know how much I love my work, but I often feel guilty for depriving my beautiful wife of quality time. We are blessed to live on this beautiful lake, and I am a very fortunate man to have the love and devotion of the most beautiful woman in Clinton County. You take excellent care of our home and provide our children love, supervision and discipline. I admit that I have been absent and negligent in that regard. This investigation was physically and emotionally draining. Perhaps it is time for me to pull the plug and retire. We could then consider travel and spending more time on *Hav-n-Fun*. Getting out from under the pile of paper that I'm now buried in, will give me incentive to retire."

Liz shook her head in the negative as she responded, "Tom, I won't get my hopes up. I know how devoted you are to the police family and I have gotten used to playing second fiddle to your career. Just be careful and feel secure knowing how much I love you. You do provide us security, keep us financially sound and display love and affection during the brief time you are with us."

Liz's emotion filled statement, inspired moisture in Tom's blue eyes. He arose from the table, gathered Liz in his arms, kissed her passionately and whispered, "You are the most precious and dear person in my life. I hope you know – and will always know – how much I love you."

Liz's eyes now glistened with moisture, as she responded, "And, you are dear and precious to me. I could not bear to lose you."

Savoring the moment and mutual commitment to love, they clung together in silence for a spell. The spell was broken as Tom whispered, "Got-ta go, my love! I anticipate another very busy day." He kissed Liz on the forehead, and stated as he headed out the door, "Now that Bashoul is locked up and we are not investigating serious crimes, I promise to start spending more time with you and our kids."

Liz's face displayed a skeptical smile as she responded, "I won't make any vacation plans in the immediate future, Mr. dedicated cop."

"Yeah, I know love," Tom called out in reply, "but I promise to be home early today. Decide where you want me to take you tomorrow night for dinner."

Tom arrived at the Plattsburgh state police station at 8:00 a.m., which was about a half hour later than his normal morning arrival time. As anticipated, Harry Standish, police reporter for the Plattsburgh-Press-Republican, and Mary Sykes, police reporter for the Albany Times-Union, were waiting in the station lobby. Tom did not recognize the third person waiting and would subsequently learn that the young, attractive blonde woman was Jeanette LeDeau, a reporter for the Montreal Gazette.

Tom did not appreciate being pestered by representatives of the media; however, his feeling of elation concerning Abdul's arrest gave warmth to his, "Good morning," greeting. He added, "Were you provided a release concerning our arrest of Omar Bashoul?"

"Yes," the three responded in unison. "However, we would appreciate some additional details."

"Well, okay, fire away; however, as prosecution of Bashoul is ongoing, I am not at liberty to discuss in depth the details of Mr. Bashoul's crimes. I would suggest you speak with District Attorney Racette concerning when he plans presentation of the crimes to the grand jury."

Standish responded, "I-we, contacted the district attorney's office and were told Mr. Racette plans to hold a press conference at 11 this morning. We plan to attend that briefing, but at last night's hearing, when Judge Morrisey ordered Bashoul to jail, Bashoul shouted out that America would feel the wrath of Allah today. Was this just an angry outburst, or should the public be on the alert for some sort of retaliation by supporters of Mr. Bashoul?"

Smiling in response, Tom responded, "I believe Omar Bashoul, is accustomed to having things go his way. He believed my nephew Jack Weston was dead and Jack's appearance in court to testify against him was a shock and surprise. He was most likely under the impression the prosecution's case against him was weak, and as 'things' didn't go as he expected, he became angry and responded by making an idle threat. Bashoul is obviously intelligent and accustomed to bullying people to achieve success. It is highly unlikely he has the where-with-all or connections to cause damage to our nation."

As Tom was answering the reporter's question, the call light on his desk top phone was flashing. Tom lifted the receiver, pushed the intercom button and said, "Hey, Bob, what's up?"

Trooper Bob Sutton, who was on station desk duty responded, "Senior you better go into the squad room and look at the TV. A plane just crashed into the World Trade Center."

"Oh, my God," Tom responded. He placed the phone receiver on its cradle, then, invited the reporters to join him in the station's squad room. As he left his office, he noted the time was 8:35 a.m.

Captain Burrows, Zone Sergeant Gibbs, Station Commander Sergeant Lewis, and all five member's of Tom's BCI squad, were in the room, and all eyes were glued on the television screen, which depicted smoke and fire in the upper floors of Manhattan's World Trade Center Tower One. Some in the room emitted an audible gasp as they watched people escaping from being burned alive, leaping from the building to a certain death.

Reports were being relayed from on-scene reporters to their station studio newscaster, who reported that it was unknown why a commercial airplane had crashed into the tower on a perfectly clear, sunny, azure blue sky – morning. It was obvious everyone in the airplane had been killed and the building had experienced extensive damage. As on scene reporting continued, newscasters speculated as to how such a horrific accident could occur. The answer soon was provided in a "special news bulletin." Another commercial airliner had just smashed into Tower Two of the World Trade Center! The horrific crash was shown live on the television screen. It was suddenly clear, these were not accidents; rather, a planned attack by terrorists on a suicide mission.

A chill travelled up Tom's spine as the news room broadcaster grimly speculated, "Is America under attack?"

In response to the chilling question, a bulletin flashed on

the screen announcing that two more planes had deviated from their assigned flight plan and were headed south. The FAA was ordering all commercial airplanes presently in flight, to land as soon as possible at the nearest airport. It was reported that President Bush had ordered scrambling of Air Force fighters to intercept the two commercial planes having deviated from their flight plans. Millions of American's watched the horrific real life drama being presented live and all were assailed by a myriad of negative emotions. It was a certainty that the majority of viewers could not accept or believe what they were seeing could happen in America. Tom's mind was awash with questions? Who are these terrorists? What is their motive? What do they hope to accomplish? What role does Bashoul have in this? These were questions racing through the minds of many citizens and anticipating recall to duty, off-duty troopers began arriving at the station. The small squad room was now filled with people and the mood was somber.

The carnage caused Tom to reflect on his visit to the state police command center located on the 49th floor of World Trade Center's Tower Two, during the years Mario Cuomo was Governor of New York. At the time, Cuomo maintained his New York City offices on the 50th floor, and the 49th floor was occupied by the state police. Tom had visited Tower Two on two separate occasions. He was awed by the majesty of the twin monoliths and like most Americans, familiar with the complex, was under the impression they were indestructible. He also knew that the World Trade Center complex was virtually a city unto itself, as thousands of folks worked for various businesses housed within the complex. There was also a plaza beneath the structures that comprised restaurants, boutiques and other shops.

A myriad of thoughts raced through his mind as he watched the carnage. *How many people will die? Oh God, how horrific! Please have mercy on all those poor souls! Thank God, the state police moved out of the building after Cuomo left the governorship. New York City police and fire department personnel are dealing with a disaster of monumental proportions! Those poor folks! What would I do if I were there?*

As Tom continued watching the carnage, Abdul's statement of the previous evening started haunting his mind. *"Tomorrow, Allah..."*

He had been wrong in his assessment of Omar Bashoul. *What role had Bashoul played in this terrorist plot? It now seems obvious Omar was somehow involved in the wanton destruction that is taking place. We will have to try to find out; however, I know it will be next to impossible to get him to reveal anything.*

Not a sound came from the group gathered in the small room, and all eyes remained fixed on the television screen. It was certain that despite the silence, every mind was awash with confusion, anger and some were engaged in silent prayer for the innocent victims of evil. It was heart-wrenching to watch, as people, who had started, what they anticipated as just another work day, now were leaping to a certain death from the upper area of the building, as an alternative to being burned alive.

All in the group gathered in the squad room – excepting the reporters – had witnessed death and destruction before, some via the military and all via their police career; however, watching so many innocent lives being lost by acts of diabolical evil, made them angry. The atmosphere in the room was tense as negative emotions filled every mind present. By the nature of their careers, it was certain that all felt frustration at not being able to aid the victims of carnage.

As a police professional and former member of the USMC, Tom was accustomed to taking action to prevent destruction, save lives and destroy the enemy. As he stared at the television screen, powerless to take action to aid in stopping the death and destruction that he was witnessing, his mind was assailed by frustration, anger, confusion, sadness and a sense of helplessness. His anger intensified as he watched the indestructible towers collapse. *Oh Dear God, how could this happen? Why did you let it happen? How many people have lost their lives and how many are injured? It is a certainty that many brave police officers and firefighters who courageously entered the towers to rescue folks will be either killed or injured.*

As a consummate police professional, he began to focus on what motivated the attack and who was responsible. *Who is responsible for what can be equated to an act of war? What was the motivation behind such evil? Where are the scumbag(s) responsible? Had Bashoul played a role in plotting this diabolical act of war? If not, he certainly knew who was responsible and could provide the answers.*

As the news coverage continued it was reported that American Airlines Flight 11, had departed Logan AA, in Boston Massachusetts, that morning, destined for California. At 8:45 a.m. Flight 11, smashed into Tower One of the World Trade Center, striking it in the vicinity of the 80th floor of the 110 story structure. Air Traffic Control advised Flight 11 left its assigned flight plan shortly after takeoff and commenced on a southward course toward New York City. When queried as to why he had changed course, the pilot did not respond. It would subsequently be learned that the concerned controllers heard a message apparently intended for the planes passengers, but broadcast over the ATC radio frequency.

The voice said, "We have some planes. Just stay quiet and you'll be okay. We are returning to the airport. Nobody move. Everything will be okay. If you try to make any moves, you'll endanger yourself and the airplane. Just stay quiet. Nobody move please. We are going back to the airport. Don't try to make any stupid moves."

That voice would subsequently be identified as Mohammed Atta, leader of the group engaged on suicide missions to kill as many Americans as possible.

At 8:45 a.m., flight 11, flying at full speed and containing 20,000 gallons of highly explosive aviation fuel, smashed into the 80th floor of Tower One of the World Trade Center, immediately killing everyone aboard the plane and sending a wave of exploding fuel throughout the upper floors of the massive structure. People were observed leaping to a certain death to avoid being burned alive.

At 9:03 a.m. it became obvious that the crash into Tower One was no accident, as United Flight 175, having also departed Logan Airport, destined for California – flying at full speed – smashed into the 60th floor area of World Trade Center's Tower Two. It would subsequently be learned that a flight attendant aboard the plane called a United Airlines mechanic and informed him the crew had been murdered and the plane hijacked.

Assailed by negative emotions, the strongest of which was rage, Tom left the squad room and returned to his office to get a notebook. Seeming totally out of character for a man recognized as a calm, cool, consummate professional, upon entering the office, he kicked the trash basket beside his desk and swore out loud, "Damn you Bashoul! You obviously had something to do with this murderous outrage! You need to be fried, and damned bleeding heart New York law prevents that from happening!"

After locating his notebook in a desk drawer, Tom returned to the squad room intent on making notations as to information pouring in from the media. Upon returning to the squad room, his eyes were greeted by smoke rising from the Pentagon, in Arlington, Virginia. He would learn that American Airlines flight

77, which had also departed Logan, destined for California, had just smashed into the Pentagon.

In subsequent news reporting, it was learned that a flight attendant aboard Flight 77, called her mother in Las Vegas, and told her the plane was being hijacked by 6 individuals. It was also learned that Flight 77 passenger Barbara Olson, had called her husband Theodore Olson, the Solicitor General of the United States. She informed her husband that the plane had been hijacked, and the hijackers were armed with knives and box cutters.

Later news reporting, subsequent to an examination of the planes passenger list by the FBI, would reveal two passengers aboard the plane; Khalid al-Mihdhar and Nawaf al-Hazmi, were on the FBI's terrorist alert list.

In the passage of just a couple of hours on a lovely early fall day, Satanic acts of evil were responsible for the loss of perhaps thousands of innocent lives and millions, perhaps billions of dollars in property destruction.

Yet, the carnage was not over! United Airlines Flight 93, which had departed Newark International Airport, with destination California, diverted from its assigned flight plan. Messages intended for passengers aboard the plane – like with Flight 11 – were mistakenly broadcast over the air traffic control frequency. "Ladies and gentlemen, this is the Captain. Please sit down. Keep remaining sitting. We have a bomb on board, so sit, uh, this is the Captain; would like you all to remain seated. There is a bomb on board and are going back to the airport – and to have our demands met. Please remain quiet."

Subsequent to this radio transmission, Flight #93 crashed in Stony Creek, Pennsylvania! The plane disintegrated on impact with the ground. All passengers aboard Flight #93 met instant death; however, no other deaths or destruction occurred.

It would subsequently be reported that brave passengers aboard Flight #93, had become aware the hijackers were on a suicide mission and fought with the hijackers, preventing them from proceeding to their intended target.

The American public would learn that acts of heroism took place aboard the plane. Flight #93 passenger Thomas Burns, Jr. told his wife over phone, "I know we're all going to die, there's three of us who are going to do something about it. I love you, honey."

Another passenger, Todd Beamer, was heard saying during the same phone call: "Are you guys ready? Let's roll!"

Tom, felt a measure of satisfaction in learning of the passengers bravery. They had prevented the terrorist hijackers from striking their intended target and in the process saved numerous innocent lives. He offered silent thanks and prayer for the heroes of Flight #93. Prayer and thanks were also extended to the 343 New York City Firefighters, 69 New York City Police officers and 2 paramedics, who gave their lives trying to rescue people.

When Tom returned to his office, there were several voice mail messages waiting for him. He listened to each, prioritized the calls and started calling each of the callers. His first call was to FBI SA Ray Forrest, who was as shocked and angry as Tom.

"Ray," Tom greeted, "at this moment, I personally want to kill that son-of-a-bitch Bashoul! He obviously has some sort of role in this murderous rampage. However, I know we would be 'whistling Dixie' to question Bashoul before we have all the intelligence concerning the plane hijackers. I presume the FBI has already commenced gathering information and evidence. When you are ready to confront Bashoul, give me a call and we will put him through the ringer. It is unlikely the pile of dog crap will tell us anything, but if you are able to build a case against him, under federal law, he will face the death penalty."

Forrest replied, "Tom, reflecting on Bashoul's verbal outburst of last evening, it does appear obvious he played some role, or at least has knowledge of who the leader is behind these outrageous suicide missions. We are already gathering intelligence as rapidly as possible and there will be hundreds of agents working 24-7 to arrest or perhaps eliminate the person, or persons, responsible. I will be in touch, or probably my supervisor will, when we are ready to move on Bashoul. I trust whatever info you come up with at your end, you will pass on."

"I definitely will Ray, and a diabolical plan is already forming in my mind."

"Oh-oh, what are you considering? We've got to keep anger in check, stay professional, and conduct our investigation within legal parameters."

"You're damned right, I am angry Ray! However, I assure you we are on the same page. Just wondering if we should plant one of 'ours' in the jail and have him snuggle up to Bashoul. You know Ali (FBI SA Ali Mahoud) put on a magnificent performance convincing Bashoul to travel to New York City, and Bashoul only heard his voice over the phone. Perhaps you might consider using Ali?"

"Hmm, that is an interesting proposal. Will give it some thought, and run it by the boss."

"Please stay in touch Ray. My next call is going to be to Scott McCormick, (RCMP Intelligence) and ask him to obtain listing of Abdul's toll calls and his business records."

"You don't have to," Ray responded, "have already reached out to Scott. It will be interesting to see who Abdul's friends and associates are."

"Good, Ray. Let's hope we end up frying this asshole!"

2

Virtually all of the prisoners in the Clinton County jail were also focused on television screens, watching the carnage, death, and destruction. Omar Bashoul was the only inmate displaying a smile as the death and destruction was taking place. He silently prayed and gave thanks to Allah, for providing the courage and strength necessary to carry out the plot that he had personally suggested to Osama, after the disappointment of 1993. The truck bomb loaded with explosives had resulted in a great deal of structural damage, but minimal death of American infidels. Mohammed Atta and his 18 compatriot warriors had carried out their suicide mission with great success. Omar offered silent prayer and praise to the Al Qaeda warriors, who were now being embraced and rewarded by Allah. However, a scowl replaced Omar's smile upon learning the plane having the White House as its target, crashed in Pennsylvania. Something had gone wrong and he would subsequently learn that passengers on the plane fought with their hijackers to regain control of the aircraft. Their resistance apparently prevented hijackers, Ziad Jarrah, Ahmed al-Haznawi, Ahmed al-Nami, and Saeed al-Ghamdi, from carrying out their diabolical plan. Regardless, the souls of these Al Qaida warriors deserved the reward of paradise.

The murder charge Omar was facing was of little concern to him; however, he now wished he had not erupted in anger the previous evening. He now knew the American authorities would suspect he was a player in the attack and would employ many different means to break him. Even while pondering this dilemma, he smiled in knowing that the American system of justice was impotent and weak, and he was more intelligent than those who would come after him. *Besides, by the time they have decided what course of action to take, I will be out of here; thanks to Allah, who provides the means. I will then arrange to leave this nation of infidels and join Osama in his Muslim enclave. However, before leaving some unfinished business needs to be taken care of. Minister Horban must be rewarded for his treachery. Also, Weston, that arrogant, cocky, state police investigator who tricked me, must be properly rewarded.*

3

Within 72 hours after the kamikaze attack upon America, the FBI, with assistance of America's intelligence agencies, had identified all of the Islamic hijackers. There were nineteen in total. Fifteen of the nineteen were citizens of Saudi Arabia (interestingly, an ally of the US). Two were from the United Arab Emirates, and one was from Lebanon. All were labeled as Al Qaeda operatives.

Incredibly, the 19 jihadists were in America legally. It was reported that Mohammed Atta was leader of the group and he, along with Marwan al-Shehhi, Ziad Jarrah, and Hani Hanjour, had been taking flight training in South Florida.

While living in the U.S., the hijackers were described by those coming in contact with them, as friendly, but loners, generally only associating with members of the Muslim community. It was also learned that the 'potential pilots' receiving training, had indicated disinterest in knowing how to land an aircraft. Why this did not raise a red flag of warning to authorities remained a mystery.

President George Bush, traveled to New York City, where he visited the Trade Center ruins, praised the emergency responders and victims of the attack and rallied American patriotism. He subsequently declared war on the Islamic terrorist group identified as Al Qaeda and advised that they would be hunted down and brought to justice. FBI SA Ray Forrest shared Tom Weston's suggestion with FBI Supervisors. There was no doubt that Omar Bashoul, aka, Abdul Markesh, either had knowledge of, or was somehow involved in the jihadist plot to seize airplanes and use them as missiles to kill Americans. However, in typical bureaucratic indecisiveness and slowness, no decision was forthcoming as to placing an Arabic speaking plant in the Clinton County jail, in an attempt to get Omar to reveal information and/or evidence about the 9/11 attacks. Hundreds of FBI agents were assigned to investigate the obvious terrorist attack by Islamic zealots, upon America, and President Bush was kept apprised as to the progress of the investigation.

A grieving nation learned that after the truck bomb attack at the World Trade Center in 1993, leaders of the radical Sunni Islamic organization known as Al Qaeda began plotting how to cripple America - kill as many Americans as possible and cause panic among the American people. The founder and leader of Al Qaeda, was identified as Osama Bin Laden, the son of a wealthy Saudi. The Muslim hijackers were Al Qaeda soldiers, imbued with hatred for America, and had committed themselves to the suicide mission that would assure them eternal bliss in paradise.

Osama Bin Laden was targeted for capture or assassination. What was not reported was that while Osama was attending King Abdulaziz University, he met one, Omar Mohammed Bashoul, an Egyptian scholar, who spoke fluent French, English and Arabic, like Bin Laden, Bashoul was an Islamic zealot, who hated America and despised Americans. The primary reason for his hatred was America's support of Israel. His father had been killed by Israeli soldiers during the Sinai 7 day war.

Bashoul envisioned Al Qaida as the means of ridding the

world of the infidels, who mocked the Koran and violated Allah's laws. Like Bin Laden, Bashoul had committed himself to the "Holy War," but he had no desire, nor inclination to sacrifice his own life in the Jihad. Instead, he would use his superior intelligence to aid Bin Laden's warriors in carrying out their mission. In 1995, Bashoul obtained a visa and traveled to Canada. Upon arrival in Canada, he commenced using the name Abdul Markesh, and set up business as 'Abdul's Specialty Store.' Abdul's Specialty was purchasing both legitimate and illegitimate items at a discount price from people seeking to get rid of the items and then re-selling the merchandise at a profit. However, whether he made a profit or not, was of little importance, for Abdul's Specialty store was merely a front to give the appearance that Abdul was a legitimate businessman. In truth, he was Osama Bin Laden's liaison to the jihadist's that would come to America. Bin Laden wired transfers of money to a Bank Corporation account in the name of Abdul Markesh, and Markesh/Bashoul, wired periodic sums of money to Mohammed Atta, who distributed the money to his cohorts.

Stan LaPierre and Jack Weston had appeared at Abdul's Specialty Store in 1999, bringing items they had recovered while diving in Lake Champlain. The items consisted of relics from the American Revolutionary War and War of 1812, such as; muskets, musket balls, swords, knives and metallic items that had adorned uniforms. Omar recognized that these items were traded to him because it was illegal to dispose of the historic items in the United States. When LaPierre and Weston appeared with gold coins bearing the mint date 1749, he immediately recognized the coins as part of the lost treasure from the French ship *Le Casconade,* which historically sank in Lake Champlain in 1751. He had heard the story about the lost treasure and knew that several chests full of gold coins had been lost. From the gist of the conversation he had with the divers concerning the gold, he recognized they had recovered the entire lost treasure, which would be worth a fortune in this day and age. Bashoul decided to steal the treasure from the divers, and kill them in the process.

Canadian Mounted Police Sergeant Scott McCormick, by request of the FBI, obtained a court order for Bashoul's phone and bank records. Scott reported that Bashoul called Mohammed Atta numerous times during the previous year. Numerous wire transfers of money followed each of the calls. This info was also passed to Senior Investigator Tom Weston, who mulled over the motive Bashoul had to obtain the French gold coins, if he was being financed by Osama Bin Laden. He decided that personal greed was what motivated Bashoul to go after the gold. After all, the gold coins had an estimated value of $15 million in American dollars, and Bashoul saw the opportunity to become a very wealthy man. Tom also decided that Bashoul was the personification of evil, held no loyalty to non-believers, and he could order the murder of another human with ease. Bashoul had also demonstrated that he held no loyalty to associates hired to do his bidding, as he had them slain after they had served their purpose. He felt this was necessary to eliminate witnesses that might possibly testify against him. After delving into Bashoul's background, authorities concluded he was border line genius, had become an Islamic scholar and soon after arrival in Montreal, Bashoul received the title of Imam, and leader of the Muslim community, attending the Khalil-a-bashul Mosque. As a linguist, fluent in Arabic, English and French, the official language of Quebec province, he was able to converse freely with all who had committed their lives to Allah and attended the Mosque. He was known to his followers as, Imam Mohammed Bashoul. An analysis of the Imam's background caused Sgt. McCormick to decide Bashoul was extremely intelligent and a dangerous psychopath.

In the belief that his radical interpretation of the Koran and castigation of non-believers might cause the authorities to investigate him, Bashoul decided to obtain an insurance policy. He had received reports that Canada's Minister of Justice, Angus Horban, had a voracious sexual appetite and an affinity for sex with young women. As a very persuasive Imam, Bashoul was able to persuade, or in some cases intimidate young Muslim women, to appease Minister Horban's appetite. As a result, Horban became Bashoul's insurance policy against police investigation and prosecution. He did not perceive the possibility that Horban would eventually cooperate with the authorities, and in typical sociopath psychology, blamed Horban for tricking him into traveling to New York, where he was arrested. Horban must be rewarded for his treachery.

Fully aware that his angry outburst of the previous evening would cause the American authorities to investigate his life and question him, he conceived a plan that would prevent them from harassing him and grant him freedom.

4

The dark colored, Ford panel truck bearing the business name, 'Hoxie Bros. Plumbing' prominently displayed on both sides, exited the Northway at Plattsburgh, turned onto Perimeter Drive and drove up beside a ten foot high chain link fence topped by razor wire. Cameras were mounted on posts at each corner of the fence. As he stopped beside the fence, driver, Ahmed Gasmani, knew from this moment on every action would be recorded on film, which was a desired part of the event that had been carefully planned.

Clinton County Sheriff's Deputy Bill Hoskin was monitoring the cameras at the command center kiosk within the Clinton County Correctional Facility, and as it was 1:30 in the morning and he had started his shift at 11, he was bored and nodding in and out of sleep. Upon noticing a truck drive up alongside the facility's security fence, he became wide awake and curious as to why the vehicle was parking there in the middle of a dark, cloudless night. His concern heightened when a subject, dressed in dark clothing, exited the rear of the truck.

The subject approached the fence and placed some sort of square shaped object beside the wire. The man then re-entered the back of the van, and the truck drove out of camera range. Deputy Hoskin adjusted the zoom on his monitor to see if he could determine what the item placed by the fence was. He knew that it was not unusual for family or friends of inmates to try to introduce contraband into the facility, and his first thought was in that regard. As the camera zoomed in the package exploded. The explosion and its accompanying flash of light stunned and temporarily blinded Deputy Hoskin. While trying to recover his vision, he reached beneath his desk and flipped a switch that activated an alarm system. This action automatically locked down the facility and at the same time, transmitted an alarm to law enforcement agencies, who would respond. At the same moment Hoskin triggered the alarm, the front gate entrance to the jail complex was torn asunder by an explosive charge. Four figures dressed in military type clothing, all armed with MP3 machine guns, rushed into the complex. One of the attackers placed a satchel containing explosives against the main door of the operations building. The resulting explosion blew away the door as well as a section of wall, and the heavily armed attackers rushed through the opening.

At this hour of night, the jail complex was manned by two sheriff deputies and five correction officers. The two deputies were wearing side arms but the Correction officers were unarmed. Shift Supervisor Sergeant Ted Hughes was cut down by a burst from an MP3, and though Deputy Hoskin raised his hands in surrender, he too, was unmercifully cut down by a hail of bullets. The remaining Correction officers took cover, hiding in tool closets or cabinets.

Plattsburgh police officers James Morrow and Jeff Oates had managed to respond quickly to Deputy Hoskin's plea for help. Unfortunately being unaware that they would confront heavy fire power, both young officers were cut down by gunfire as they drove into the jail parking lot. They never got the opportunity to exit their police cruiser, and had no opportunity to flee. The police cruiser crashed into the fence of the facility and came to a stop. Both officers lay dead in the front seat of the cruiser

Omar Muhammed Bashoul, was lying on the bunk in his cell when the initial explosion was heard. He arose from the bunk with a sardonic smile displayed on his face. He spoke aloud, "Allah's legions have arrived and infidels are dying! Praise be; to Allah!" He began gathering his meager belongings and stuffed them into a duffel bag.

Bashoul's escape from the Clinton County Jail, where he was confined pending trial, for the murder of Stan LaPierre and attempted murder of Jack Weston, had been carefully planned by Bashoul and his associates. The plan purposely included violence, death and destruction to anger and demoralize the infidels who dared to think they could imprison and punish a Lion of Islam. Time was now of the utmost importance and Bashoul's only enemy, as he knew a horde of police officers would respond to the emergency alarm, triggered by Hoskin. The van left the scene of destruction and drove north on Route 22. Two miles up the road, the van turned right on Miner Farm Road, drove up alongside a white panel truck, boldly emblazoned with the words, 'Harmon's Dry Cleaners', and stopped. The occupants of the dark van used in the assault, quickly exited that truck and piled into the white panel truck. The white truck then drove to the Chazy Boat Landing, on the west shore of Lake Champlain. So far, the escape plan was going well. No police cars were observed and during the twenty minutes it took to arrive at the boat landing, the assault team shed ski masks and combat style clothing, which would be thrown into Lake Champlain.

As van driver, Ishtar Ishmani, approached the boat landing, he alternated the truck's headlights from low to high beam twice – the designated signal to accomplices waiting in a boat – then pulled to a stop alongside the dock. As soon as the truck stopped, Bashoul and those who would accompany him leapt out of the van and clambered aboard the boat. Thirty seconds later the 24 foot Stingray boat bearing the name "Fast and Loose" roared away from the dock and headed across the lake, arriving at Benson's Cove in Vermont twenty minutes later. The group could have proceeded north on the lake and into Canada; however, Bashoul had considered the possibility New York law enforcement would immediately alert Canadian authorities about the escape, and entering Canada via any point of entry would be risky. Instead, he cleverly planned for the group to separate on arrival in Vermont. Three cars had been parked for their use at the boat landing. The group, two members in each car, would then depart in ten minute intervals and drive to New Hampshire, where others awaited their arrival in a rented cabin. Bashoul planned to stay in the cabin until he arranged safe travel into Canada. The cabin was stocked with provisions for an extended stay. He had selected devoted members of his Mosque who held Canadian citizenship to conduct the raid, and as the identity of the raiders on the jail was unknown, they would have no problem crossing into Canada. He knew the authorities focus would be on him, and they would not recognize him when the time was right.

Bashoul could have arranged to leave the American continent without returning to Montreal; however, he needed to retrieve his most sacred Quran which he kept under lock and key when he was not preaching from it. This copy of the sacred teachings of Mohammed, had originally belonged to his Grandfather, and came to him via his father. He had made a solemn promise to his father that he would hold this treasure in utmost reverence and that it would forever remain in the Bashoul family. At the present time the most cherished book was inside a locked cabinet in his office at Khalil Mosque. It would be safe there until he was able to depart the land of infidels. He dared not leave it in Canada, for fear it would fall into the wrong hands and Allah would punish him for not protecting it. After retrieving the holy book, he would board a vessel in the Saint Lawrence River, which would eventually transfer him to another vessel, which would take him to Pakistan. Of course it would be necessary to create a false trail for the law enforcement hounds hunting for him. He would also have to disguise his identity and neither of these tasks would be difficult for a man of his intellect; exceptionally gifted with a devious and clever mind.

Having dropped his passengers at the boat landing, Ishtar drove casually away. He planned to return the rented panel truck to the rental agency at Albany Airport. He would then board a flight that would take him to Montreal, where he would eventually celebrate with Imam Bashoul and his comrades. As he made his way down Route 87 toward Albany, he was very careful not to violate the speed limit. It was 2:30 in the morning and there was little traffic on the well travelled interstate highway connecting Canada and the United States.

As the Northway snaked its way through the Adirondack Mountains, during the day, travelers were treated to a lovely, relaxing view of the mountains, lakes and forest. Night travelers were cautioned to watch for deer and an occasional black bear crossing the highway. However, the driver of the van bearing the business name Harmon Bros. Dry Cleaners, prominently displayed, was not interested in the beauty of the mountains or scenery. His focus was on arriving at the airport and returning to Montreal. After exiting the Northway, Ishtar drove into a pull-off near the airport entrance, removed the Velcro backed signs from the van and stuffed them in a trash barrel.

5

T om was roused from sleep by the 'instrument of torture' aka, telephone. He anticipated that this was not a pleasant call, and answered, "What now?"

Sergeant Lewis, responded, "Tom, all hell is breaking loose! Bashoul has escaped from the County jail! Sheriff Deputies were murdered and two Kingston police officers are dead! Don't have a lot of information yet, and the damned phone here is ringing off the hook. I alerted Troop Headquarters, the Border patrol and Canadian authorities. Road blocks have been established throughout the area and the border has been temporarily closed. I was assured that every vehicle crossing into Canada will be searched. We don't have a lot of info to go on, and the assholes responsible for springing Bashoul, destroyed the jail's surveillance equipment. They obviously used explosives and it appears they were armed with machine guns. What do you suggest we do that hasn't already been initiated?"

Tom was now wide awake and shaking his head in anger and disbelief. "Oh my God, I never dreamed this would happen! Who was killed in the attack?"

"Sheriff's Sergeant, Ted Hughes, Deputy Bill Hoskins, Plattsburgh Police Officers, James Morrow, and Jeff Oates, were killed. I personally knew them all. They were all good men and fine police officers. Correction officers Birney, George, Martinson and Lane, hid in the jail complex and fortunately were not injured. They are very-shaken, but professionalism kicked in and they reported to our patrol that the raiders apparently arrived in some sort of truck and they blew open the front gate to gain entrance. They do not know how many were involved in the assault on the jail; however, Correction Officer Randall Birney, reports that he was hiding in a cabinet holding cleaning equipment and trying his best to see through slotted vents in the door. He managed to observe one of the attackers as he passed by the cabinet and that individual was dressed in dark military type clothing and wearing a black ski mask."

"Mike, have you called out any of my squad?"

"Yes. Czech had advised that he was on-call investigator tonight. I called him ASAP. He is presently en-route to the jail complex and told me via radio to call you."

"Where is the crime scene command post?"

"Major O'Neill was contacted by Captain Burrows, and he directed that our command post be established at the Plattsburgh barracks. The TC (troop commander) has ordered return to duty by all Troop B members, so this place is soon going to become a mad house. I've already got the media pestering me, as does Sheriff Benson and Plattsburgh Police Chief Reeves. So far, we are holding them at bay, but when the major media gets wind of this, we are going to be deluged with media. TC has already directed that all media inquiries be directed to Captain Burrows."

"How about the victim's families, Mike, have they been contacted?"

"The Sheriff is taking care of his end and Chief Reeves is taking care of his end."

"Mike, I know you are up to your ears in ringing telephones and radio traffic at the moment, so I will contact the rest of my squad. I will check in by radio when I leave my house. I hope you had a Trooper come in to help you on the desk?"

"Trooper Dermody is on his way in Tom. We will be fine at this end and if anything new pops, I will give you a shout."

Tom concluded, with the encouragement, "Hang tough Mike," then, he hung up the phone.

Tom was pleased that 18-year veteran, Sergeant Mike Lewis, was working the desk, because Mike was a consummate professional and could keep his cool. Like Tom, Mike had served in the marines, and in fact was a Purple Heart recipient, from being wounded in Vietnam. The 45-year old was also married to a Vietnamese spitfire, and they had six children. Mike had a picture prominently displayed on his home office wall, depicting a tall, lean, smiling Marine having a dark crew-cut, standing beside two Vietnamese children. Having reached middle-age, Lewis maintained a trim physique, minus the crew cut. He had the habit of pointing to his bald pate and telling his work-mates "see this is what happens when you lead a clean life and try to keep up with the shenanigans of six kids."

Upon concluding his conversation with Sergeant Lewis, Tom called Investigators Patty Hermione, Enrico Martinez, Bill Whalen and Vic LaPlante. Fortunately, all were home and answered their phones. He furnished each a synopsis of Bashoul's escape and directed all but "Red" Whalen to proceed to the Clinton County jail and assist Investigator Ed Czech. Whalen was directed to report to the Plattsburgh station and prepare to commence duties as 'Scribe.'

Tom felt blessed to work with a group of dedicated police professionals. The Plattsburgh BCI squad was considered 'family' and every member of the family could be counted on to perform at their best. The group of five investigators admired and respected their boss, Senior Investigator Tom Weston, as he worked alongside them and made no impossible demands of them. They also appreciated the fact that the boss would support and defend them from unwarranted discipline from other supervisors. The group behaved like family, worked together as a family and celebrated birthdays, special occasions and victory over crime, as family. As a matter-of-fact, Tom's wife, often criticized her husband for being more aligned with and spending more time with his workmates than his nuclear family.

Ed "Wreck" Czech, age 31, standing 6'5' and weighing in at 240 lbs, was the largest member of the squad. He was two inches taller than his boss and outweighed Tom by about 25 lbs. Though physically imposing, the seven year state police veteran had a friendly oval shaped face and warm brown eyes. Ed sported a dark crew cut and was meticulous in maintaining its height at three inches. Many uniform troopers earned promotion to the BCI by the number of traffic tickets they issued; however, Czech had earned his promotion via his large number of criminal arrests. Ed aspired to become a member of the Bureau of Criminal Investigation early in his career and to get noticed, often stopped into the BCI office and offered to assist with investigations. As a result, he endeared himself with members of the BCI, but received constant chastisement from uniform supervisors to spend more time on the highway issuing traffic tickets.

Czech was not married, had never been married and enjoyed, as he referred to it, "playing the field."

Ed earned the moniker "Wreck," while a uniform trooper. One evening, while on patrol, he was directed to respond to a bar fight at a tavern frequented by members of the Akwesasne Indian Reservation. Ed entered the bar with 'night stick' (baton) in hand, and found two large Indian males, fighting with two members of a motorcycle gang. To gain their attention, Ed slammed his nightstick on the oak bar top, which equated to the sound of a shotgun being fired. As a result, most patrons in the bar opted to leave; however, the four highly intoxicated combatants decided to turn on the trooper. This proved to be a bad mistake. Ed skillfully used his stick to break arms and kneecaps, dropping all four to the floor, where they writhed in pain. Realizing he only had one set of handcuffs, Ed handcuffed the two Indians together, removed a whip from the bar wall, where it had adorned a picture of some unknown cowboy, and used the whip to tie the two bikers together. When the scene was secure, Ed radioed for assistance and an ambulance to respond. While waiting for help to respond, Ed purchased a draft beer from the bar owner - who was practically in tears as he gazed at smashed tables and chairs strewn about the premises - righted a bar stool and sat 'wetting his whistle' to cool down. When the troops arrived, upon entering the bar, the Sergeant accompanying the group remarked, "Damn, did you wreck this place Ed?"

"Hey Sarge," Ed responded, "As a Trooper I'm sworn to maintain peace and enforce the law. I did the best I could under the circumstances."

The bar owner then assured the Sergeant that the Trooper was not responsible for the damage and pointed to the four miscreants on the floor, two of whom were snoring and the other two moaning.

Maintaining the peace and enforcing the law that evening gained Ed the moniker, "Wreck," which caused smiles because it rhymed with Czech.

Investigator Patty Hermione, age 30, was an 8-year veteran of the state police. Patty was the smallest member of the Plattsburgh BCI squad, seemingly the antithesis of Ed Czech, standing 5' 4" and weighing in at about 115 pounds. As a strikingly beautiful brunette, with dark brown eyes, people often asked her if she were Demi Moore's twin sister. This question invoked a scowl and the response, "I am not a phony GI Jane." Men who worked with her and knew her well were quick to point out that as an exercise fanatic and possessing a Black Belt in karate, Patty was the real deal. Patty was not married and several Troopers had tried to win her affection, only to be rewarded with frustration. However, during the investigation to capture Omar Bashoul, for the murder of Stan LaPierre, she was teamed with a tall, handsome Investigator by the name of Troy Rasmussen, who worked out of troop headquarters, and he caused her heart to flutter. She and Troy had commenced dating and were considering marriage.

Ed "Wreck" Czech often remarked that Patty was the only member of the squad who could kick his butt. He enjoyed telling fellow troopers about the night the squad was celebrating the apprehension of a murder suspect. They were gathered at Crickets Bar in Peru, and partying hard. He decided to enjoy a cigar and removed an expensive Cuban cigar from his jacket pocket. As he was unwrapping the cigar, Patty informed him that cigar smoke was disgusting and warned him to put it away. Ed smiled impishly, in return, put the cigar in his mouth and lit up. Suddenly, the cigar flew from his mouth and sailed across the room. Without warning and quick as a flash, Patty had kicked the cigar from his mouth, somehow only removing the cigar and not breaking his jaw. "She is one tough little woman 'Wreck' explained. "As a matter-of-fact, she scares me enough that I don't refer to her using the word 'Broad,' for fear she will invite me outside for an education in the use of respectful terminology."

Investigator Victor "Vic" LaPlante, age 38, had been a member of the state police for 15 years, and a member of the Bureau of Criminal Investigation for 7-years. He was a transplanted French-Canadian, and spoke fluent French. As Plattsburgh was only about 25 miles south of the Canadian-Quebec border, he was a valuable asset to the squad. Most of the French province

Canadian citizens spoke both English and French; however, on occasion, some wise ass suspect from Quebec would pretend they didn't speak or understand English, only French. On those rare occasions Tom would sic Vic on them. LaPlante was about 6-feet tall, had a slim build and one of his most memorable features were intense, dark brown eyes. Vic sported a goatee, which caused his workmates to refer to him as 'The Professor.' Vic was also considered the 'mentally strong, silent' member of the squad and often while sitting at his desk pondering something, appeared to be staring into space. Vic was about two years into his second marriage to Trooper Briana, nee, Thomas; they had no children, and resided in Morrisonville. The divorce from his first wife was a bitter battle, as they fought over custody of two children. In the end, Vic, gave up the fight.

Investigator Enrico 'Rico' Martinez, age 27, had been in the state police 5-years and gained promotion to the BCI after completing only 4-years as a uniform trooper. When asked how he gained promotion so quickly he replied, "Hey, I was fortunate to enter the state police at a time when the 'job' needed minorities to boost its image with the federal government. Although my heritage is from south of the border, I was born and raised in the North Country and I don't speak Spanish, but, I certainly am not going to complain. I set my goal on gaining promotion to the BCI as quickly as possible, and now I am a happy camper."

Having dark, curly hair, dark eyes, a trim build and only an inch taller than Patty combined with having a Hispanic surname, lent credibility to minority status.

Rico was single and going steady with Trooper Michelle Barnes, who also worked out of the Plattsburgh station.

Rico was known for having a jocular personality and loved to play tricks on his workmates, who sometimes didn't appreciate them. However, Rico was loyal to his co-workers, the state police, and worked very hard on case assignments.

Rico's father had passed away when he was quite young and he was raised by his mother. After being assigned to the Plattsburgh BCI unit, he was determined to gain respect from his boss and succeeded in this regard. As a result, Rico began to envision Tom Weston as the father figure that he could call on for advice and assistance.

Investigator William 'Bill'aka 'Red' Whalen, age 35, was the 5th member of the Plattsburgh BCI unit and had been in the state police 13 years. Unlike the other members of the squad, 'Red' always wore a business suit to work.

Having a thin build, curly red hair, blue eyes and a pale face peppered with freckles, earned him the moniker "Red." Red was the most educated member of the squad, possessing a Master's degree in Criminal Justice, which he had attained while working as a Trooper and attending college on a part time basis.

Red was also referred to as 'Our attorney in residence.' This title came about due to the way Red dressed and the fact he possessed the organizational skills lacking in most gung-ho, 'damn the torpedoes' full speed ahead Troopers. Red was meticulous when it came to detail and wrote excellent reports. Consequently, Tom usually assigned Red the duty of 'case scribe' when the entire squad was involved in a heavy caper.

Red was married to Peru school teacher, Colleen nee, O'Malley - a lovely American-Irish lass - who, was appreciated at parties because after polishing off a few bottles of Guiness, would climb atop a table and perform an Irish jig. Red and Colleen had no children and lived in the Village of Peru.

Of course all of the telephone activity awoke Liz, and as she listened to her husband's conversation, and his calls recalling investigators to work, she began to worry and her face filled with alarm. Her voice was strained as she asked, "Oh Tom, what now? I gather from those phone conversations that something dreadful has happened."

Tom had immediately recognized that his wife would be concerned and placed an arm around her while he was talking on the phone. He gave her a smile – which she recognized as false - intended to reassure her that all was okay. After completion of his calls, he answered her questions first with a kiss, then holding her in his arms, he whispered, "Bashoul has escaped from jail and two sheriff's deputies and two police officers were killed during the escape. Hon, I've got to go and I don't know how long I will be gone. Hopefully, Bashoul will be recaptured before he gets very far. It is okay my love! I will be all right, and I will arrange protection for Jack. Let those worry lines disappear from your beautiful face. I've got to get going Love! Try to think positive thoughts and get some rest. Our kids will be expecting the usual smiles, laughter and love from their mother in the morning. Give them a hug and kiss for me."

Not bothering to shave, Tom quickly dressed; selecting dark slacks, a white dress shirt, minus tie, and mauve colored sports jacket. In his rush he forgot to comb his hair, but he did grab a small bottle of orange juice from the 'fridge' and poured a 'to go' mug of coffee to take with him. Realizing it might be hours before he would eat again, he quickly toasted a bagel, and slathered it with butter. He opted to take the bagel with him. While holding the bagel in one hand, he wiped his mouth with the other and gave Liz a kiss on her forehead. As he turned away he encouraged, "Stay strong Honey. 'We' will recapture Bashoul and make things right again." Then he was out the door. Upon getting in his bureau car, he looked in the rear-view mirror to back out of the drive, and realized his uncombed hair gave him the appearance of a drunk. This caused him to hesitate long enough to find the comb in his pocket and tidy up his appearance.

After backing onto Lakeshore Drive, he keyed his radio mike and called in service. During the approximate four mile drive from home to office, his ears were assailed by radio chatter. He thought, *poor Mike, if he had hair, he would be tearing it out right now.*

It would be impossible for Liz to return to sleep, as her mind was full of horrible thoughts. *Oh my God! The monster that murdered Stan and nearly killed Jack has killed again and is roaming free. He obviously holds deep hatred for my husband. Will he try to take revenge on Tom? What if he attacks our family?* She arose from bed, fell to her knees beside the bed, buried her face in her hands and commenced praying for the safety of her family and the man she loved dearly. She continued praying for approximately a half-hour, then arose, walked to her dressing table and examined herself in the mirror. The information she had just learned caused worry lines on her normally smooth face. *Got to stay strong,* she told herself. While rubbing skin conditioner on her face, and combing her dark hair, she commenced praying again, *Please Dear Lord, protect my husband and bless the families of the officers killed!* Now fully awake, with mind spinning in worry and confusion, she donned a robe, went downstairs, poured herself a cup of coffee and sat at the dining room table. While sipping black coffee, she stared out the dining room window, seeking the solitude of 'her' lake to soothe the turmoil in her mind. However, no moon or stars were visible and the lake was shrouded in darkness. She arose from the table and went out on the deck to listen to the lake. The soft sound of gentle waves being pushed ashore by a cool fall breeze gradually caused her anxiety to dissipate. She would remain on the deck for the remainder of the night and by the time the sun announced the arrival of a new day, she was at peace.

The Plattsburgh state police station was buzzing with activity, and Tom had to search for a parking spot. *This is not going to be good. Got to keep my cool and try to keep everybody organized.* He was surprised to be greeted by silence and questioning looks from the crowd of police officers already gathered. He nodded in greeting and entered his office to find Troop BCI Captain Harold Sampson, seated at his desk. The Captain was in the process of gathering information from the group of police officials gathered in the room. Sampson acknowledged Tom's arrival with a nod of his head, then, asked everyone in the small office to "Go get a cup of coffee while I speak with Weston." Realizing the request was actually an order, everyone left the office. After they departed, Sampson – displaying a tired and concerned look on his 50-year old, normally cheerful face, said, "Tom, during my 28 years in the state police, I have experienced a lot of horrible crap and investigated some tough cases, but what happened tonight tops them all. That Son-of-a-bitch Bashoul is the worst of the lot and a royal pain in the ass. Good men, fine police officers, family men, were brutally murdered tonight, because we failed to recognize how evil Bashoul truly is. Mind you, I am not blaming you or anyone in particular. You conducted your investigation regarding LaPierre's murder, as well as the attempted murder of your nephew, by the book, but I believe immediately after the terrorist attack on the 11th; in light of Bashoul's threat the previous evening, we should have immediately moved him to a higher security facility. Unfortunately that did not happen, and we are now up to our eyeballs in death and destruction. What do you suggest we focus on now to capture the scumbag?"

"Well sir," Tom replied, "we share the same feelings. I was remiss in not giving any thought to the possibility that Bashoul would try to escape from our county jail. After all, it is a relatively new facility and had all the latest security devices and measures in place. On September 11, I spoke with FBI Special Agent Ray Forrest, and told him that as it was reasonable to believe Bashoul, played some sort of role in the attacks that took place. I suggested that the 'Feebs' place SA Ali Mahoud, in the Clinton County jail with Bashoul. As you know, Mahoud is a native of Saudi Arabia, and fluent in Arabic. My plan was to have Mahoud gain Bashoul's confidence and pretend he also hated America and considered Americans infidels. Though Mahoud was instrumental in aiding our arrest of Bashoul, they did not personally meet and only conversed by phone. I thought it might work. Forrest said he would run my suggestion past his supervisor. The FBI then procrastinated and in typical, "we are now in charge and don't want you meddling in our investigation," didn't use Mahoud, and to date, had not confronted Bashoul. I guess they were hopeful of capturing someone connected to the jihadists that would rat out Bashoul. Apparently, they haven't been successful in that regard. But then again, they (FBI) have not been forthright and friendly since 9/11.

I believe Bashoul will seek some means to leave America, and seek refuge in an Islamic country. As we have no idea where he was headed, or in which direction he went after escaping, our best course of action would be to monitor all airports and ports, to watch for him. Of course gotta believe the 'Feebs' are already doing that. We should also provide his physical description, accompanied by his arrest photo to all media outlets. We need to get everyone interested in aiding us to capture him. The release should also include provision of a large monetary reward for information leading to his arrest."

Troop B Commander Major Chris O'Neill entered the office while his BCI Captain and Senior Investigator were conversing. He waved a hand to indicate the two remain seated, then stood leaning against a wall, while listening to their conversation. The

Major rubbed his chin, while contemplating Tom's suggestion, nodded his head in agreement, then asked, "Knowing what an evil bastard he is, do you think he poses a risk to Jack, or any of the folks he feels betrayed him?"

Shaking his head in the negative, Tom answered, "He will not personally get involved, because he is not one to personally get his hands dirty. He would also consider the heightened risk of being caught, if one of his agents was apprehended. However, he is the personification of evil and, as a respected Imam in the Islamic faith very likely has many devoted followers, who are imbued with hatred for infidels. With your permission, I will assign security to Jack."

"That is a given, Tom, and make sure you assign two tough Troopers."

Tom smiled as he responded, "I am considering assigning Patty Hermione and Troy Rasmussen. You know Sir they handled that attempt on Jack's life at CVPH, very well."

"Good choice. What about yourself? He (Bashoul) has to be really pissed at you for scamming him into travelling to New York City. He could very likely seek revenge."

"I appreciate your concern, Sir. However, I don't believe he will concern himself with me, and you know I am able to take care of myself."

"Yes, but what about your family? God forbid the Scum Sucker would want to harm Liz, or your kids, but we both know Bashoul is an evil, diabolical bastard."

The Major's statement triggered a look of concern on Tom's face. It was a legitimate question and he remained silent for a moment as he pondered that possibility. He finally replied, "Sir, would it be too costly to provide security for my family – just until Bashoul is captured?" He quickly added, "I would prefer the bastard was killed."

"No, Tom, and in reflecting on our justice system, I would hope for – and I know as a police professional I shouldn't suggest this – that we send the bastard to his desired liaison with virgins. That is apparently the ultimate goal of all the nut job Islamic jihadists. For some strange reason their God and their Holy Book, encourage violence toward non-believers and they have a warped perception of right and wrong. It seems totally perverted to believe murdering another human being ensures them of going to their heaven. And, what causes them to believe that they will be rewarded with a bevy of virgins when they arrive there?"

As the Major spoke Tom nodded in silent agreement and replied, "A while back curiosity about the Islam religion caused me to read the Quran and a book titled, 'The Life and Times of Mohammad' authored by a Catholic Priest and published in 1919. As you are probably aware, the Quran is composed of 'Suras' purporting to be revelations given to Mohammad by the Archangel Gabriel. Many of the passages in the Quran are confusing and don't make sense. It was an eye opener to learn that Mohammad was illiterate and that his revelations were written by others many years after his death. Also an eye opener to learn that during his 61 years of life, Mohammad, had 13 wives. Islam consists of two religious factions. One is 'Sunni' and the other Shiite. They are in conflict with each other and their differences often lead to violent conflict. Radical Islamic factions believe that all non-believers must be either: converted, enslaved or killed. In my mind, it seems incredibly perverse that Allah, the God they revere, is a vengeful deity that condones, rape, torture and murder; whereas our Christian God, advocates peace, love and forgiveness. The philosophy of the two deities totally clash and have resulted in death and destruction for centuries. It is a sad indictment against all of mankind that a clash in religious beliefs has resulted in warfare for some 1500 years and the death of millions of people. Sir, I believe radical Islamic jihadists are hell-bent on destroying Christianity and democracy, with the intent of establishing a worldwide structure of Islamic theocracies. This is the goal of Osama Bin Laden and appears to be the goal of Omar Mohammed Bashoul. There is no hope of converting Islamic zealots into becoming peace loving citizens. Putting them in prison when they commit crimes is not going to accomplish anything other than making them more hateful. They must be destroyed! Sorry, for my rant, but this is one Roman Catholic who does not want my heirs or great-grandchildren wearing 'hijabs and thobes, and praying five times a day to a vengeful God."

Major O'Neill and Captain Samson listened to Tom's tirade and when he finished, shook their heads in agreement. "The hell of it is," O'Neill responded, "money motivates every issue and the leaders of the free world, including America, snuggle up to the Imam's and Mullah's because of oil. The world media is gradually being infiltrated by Muslims and it seems every time a Muslim goes on a murderous rampage, certain members of the media and political leaders portray the horrific event as an 'isolated incident' by an extremist. Those 'isolated incidents' number in the hundreds. With what is occurring frequently throughout Europe - which is being inundated by Muslims - and now in America, a hell-of-a lot of people are being slaughtered by random Islamic extremists. The murderous rampage of just a couple of weeks ago should be a wake-up call to America and the free world. Now, our military is about to become mired down in a God-forsaken hell hole by the name of Iraq and thousands of our fine troops will die as a result of having to wait until fired upon because their enemy does not wear an identifiable uniform and all Iraqi's look alike. What a mess, and now we face the challenge of nailing this Bashoul nut job before he kills more innocent folks.

"Tom, as you can see, we are on the same page and I am as frustrated as you."

Captain Samson's only comment was, "Gentlemen, I agree."

Major O'Neill asked his Captain to remain supervising the command post while he and Tom went to the County jail.

"Let's slip out the back door of the station," the Major suggested, "to avoid the crowd of media people waiting in the lobby, and go meet with 'our people' (SP) at the jail. I would like to personally see the scene of devastation. I will ride with you."

Tom informed Red Whalen, that he and the TC were going to the county jail complex. "Red, I am leaving you to hold down the office. Be prepared to become deluged with information. If you can't keep up with it, let me know and I will assign some help."

"Thanks, Boss, but you know I am the fastest two finger typist in the east, and I can handle it."

Tom followed Major O'Neill out the back door of the Plattsburgh station. To take their mind off what they were about to confront, as well as the stress of anticipated duties, during the 15 minute ride to the jail complex, they engaged in conversation about family and sports. On arrival, they were greeted by a phalanx of police who had their hands full trying to prevent media personnel and members of the public, from violating the crime scene. Being well known to the local police community, Tom was immediately recognized, and directed to park in front of the ribbon of yellow tape that bordered the crime scene. Not wanting to taint any evidence, the two waited for a trooper to meet them and escort them through the complex. Tom was relieved to see their escort would be Investigator Enrico Martinez.

The normally happy-go-lucky investigator, displayed a grim look and cautioned, "A scene from Hell, Boss! The command-control center was destroyed by some sort of high explosive, and Deputies Hughes and Hoskin, armed only with issue side arms, did not have the means to stop the assault. Both were executed and both were hit by multiple rounds. The attackers only focus was apparently to spring Bashoul, because, no other prisoners are missing. Correction officers, Birney, Martinson and Lane, survived by hiding in utility cabinets, they are presently on their way down to our station for debriefing. Patty is driving them down."

"What about Bashoul's cell," Tom inquired? "Anything of interest found in there?"

"Nope, not a thing, he apparently took any apparel, books, or writing material with him."

"Where - were the Plattsburgh officers killed," Major O'Neill asked?

"Just outside the front gate, Sir, it is probable to believe they were cut down by whoever was waiting for Bashoul and the assault team. They were both cut to ribbons by automatic gunfire, before they exited their cruiser. The Coroner was here and they have been taken to the morgue. The cruiser was towed to Plattsburgh PD, and I was told it is being covered with a canvas. It will be available there for processing by our identification bureau."

"Any witnesses," Tom asked?"

"Only the three correction officers and a handful of prisoners; as previously indicated, the CO's hid out in utility cabinets and those inmates who saw the attackers, told me there were four or five attackers, dressed in dark military type clothing and wearing dark ski masks. They heard the explosions, but did not witness the killing of the guards."

"Thanks Rico," Tom responded. "Stay here and assist the forensic guys. When they are done, report to the command post."

"See ya there, Boss," Enrico answered.

Major O'Neill and Tom were glum during their return to the Plattsburgh station. O'Neill broke the silence, and he spoke in a strained, quiet whisper, "These were senseless killings, Tom. Those men leave families that are now grieving. We must honor them and do our best to provide solace for their families. I will arrange for an SP honor guard at each of their services."

"Yes, Sir," Tom responded, in an equally quiet tone, "and I will say prayers that their souls have been welcomed into Heaven. I will also pray that their families recover quickly from the sudden shock of losing their loved one. I believe Liz, will visit their widows and offer them assistance."

As they approached the Plattsburgh station, the Major placed a hand on Tom's arm and said in a voice strained with emotion, "You know Tom, as professionals we are expected to deal with death, violence and destruction without displaying emotion. I don't know about you, but suppressing the turmoil boiling inside of me right now, is difficult. After all, though we wear the grey uniform that symbolizes strength and authority, we are still human and hiding our emotions in a closet has caused many of our brothers to seek relief via 'the bottle.' I have seen many fine 'Brothers' destroy their police career and lose their family, due to alcoholism. We have got some difficult days ahead of us, Tom, and I know I can count on you and every member of your unit – every member of this troop - to perform at their very best. I am concerned that this investigation will take a toll on everyone, because they will exhaust themselves in our effort to nab that S.O.B., Bashoul. I appreciate their devotion to duty; however, I do not want folks exhausting themselves in the process. Please direct your squad to get adequate sleep and spend time with their families. That includes you Tom. I know you well, and when a serious crime occurs, you are a tenacious hound dog, entirely focused on capturing the fox. Bashoul, will eventually make a mistake, Tom, and we will snare him. Please don't exhaust yourself and find time for your family. Oh, and encourage your squad to lay off the booze during this time of turmoil. When this nightmare is over, we will celebrate. As a matter-of-fact, though I am not a big drinker, I plan to get very drunk when Bashoul is either in chains, or dead!"

"You and I think alike and share the same concerns, Sir. It saddens me to see so many of our SP family try to seek relief from the stress of the job via a bottle. Alcoholism is the most prevalent illness of our profession and it has ruined marriages and destroyed careers. Many fine Troopers, unable to find relief, committed suicide. I am thankful that many careers, marriages and lives have been saved via an excellent rehabilitation program. I will do my best to convince my devoted crew to get adequate sleep and lay off the booze, while we work this case. They will be looking forward to celebrating with you when this is over."

An awakening sun was pushing away the darkness on the east shore of Lake Champlain, as the two arrived at the station. As they exited the car and made their way into the rear door of the building, Major O'Neill muttered, "Damned piranha, (media) have filled the front driveway. I hope Burrows is keeping them at bay."

Every commissioned officer in Troop B was waiting in the squad room, and most greeted their Troop Commander with a snappy salute.

"At ease men," Major O'Neill responded. "No need for formalities at this time and place. However, I need your complete attention to detail and would greatly appreciate any suggestions this pool of expertise has that will facilitate and expedite the apprehension of the despicable pile of human crud responsible for what amounts to an act of war."

As the Major was addressing his officers, Tom went into the BCI squad room. Investigator Red Whalen was the only person in the room. Red waved one hand and called out, "Hi boss!"

Tom responded, "Red has anyone reported in with any helpful information?"

"Troopers Jerry Mack and Dick Thomas found a black Ford van truck parked alongside Miner Farm Road. The truck is registered to Hoxie Brothers Plumbing, in Ellenburg (NY). I called business owner Bud Hoxie, and he said his truck had been stolen sometime after 11 p.m. last night. Troops had the truck towed into the Chazy station, for securing and processing by our forensic guys. Investigator Martinez is on his way up to Ellenburg to interview Hoxie. Mack and Thomas told me there was nothing immediately obvious to indicate this was the truck used by the jail attackers. We will have to see what the i.d. (forensic) guys turn up. No other leads boss."

"Did they search the area around the truck?"

"Yes, and came up blank."

Tom re-entered the station squad room and reported what he had just been told to the officers. There was a murmur from the group indicating they were hopeful fingerprints or other evidence, were found in the examination of the truck. Major O'Neill advised that Captain Burrow's had been assigned as media liaison officer. He would hold his first press briefing at 9:00 a.m. and promised to update the media as new information was developed.

"Good man to handle that horrible job, Sir." Tom acknowledged. "Dealing with the media has always been that aspect of our work that I hate the most. Some are okay; however, all too many are a royal pain-in-the-ass. They have no clue how important it is to protect and preserve a crime scene and even if they did, they could care less. They are like vampires that thrive on blood, gore and sensationalism – sadly because a large segment of our society does too." Having vented this feeling, he added, "I am going down to the morgue to examine the victims with Doc Hartigan. Anyone want to join me?"

None of the officers verbally responded; however, their facial expressions were indicative that none were interested.

Turning his attention to Major O'Neill, Tom said, "Hopefully, when I return to the command post I will have some information that will take us out of the dead-end we have reached so far."

'Coroner for life,' Doctor Horatio Hartigan, was a reputable pathologist in the medical forensic fraternity and a respected member of the Plattsburgh community. Having a substantially round body, jovial appearing face; head as shiny as a cue ball, and sporting small black framed, round spectacles, worn on the tip of a nose seemingly to small for his face, gave folks the impression he was more suited to be a comedian than a medical doctor. Doc was usually attired in a rumpled suit, having the appearance of having been slept in, which seemed to lend credence to that mistaken impression. In truth, Doctor Hartigan was a consummate professional, and while engaged in his ghoulish work wore a white smock that hid his unkempt appearance. Doc 'Ratio' as he was referred to by police, loved associating with members of the law enforcement community and he actually enjoyed engaging in verbal combat with defense attorneys when on the witness stand. Most local attorneys had learned their lesson from being made fools of by Coroner Hartigan, and did not attempt to trip him up.

Doc had already completed examination and autopsied the four police officers, when Tom arrived in the morgue. Troop B forensic specialist and member of the troop's identification bureau, Claire Martin, was present, had taken photographs during the autopsies and gathered evidence consisting of blood, hair and bone tissue. Claire was 30-years old and had entered the New York State Police as a civilian employee, after graduating from medical school at age 25. Both of her parents were medical doctors; her dad a pathologist and her mother, an internist, at Presbyterian Medical in NYC. As the only child of the Martin's,

Claire became fascinated with the 'study of death,' as her father referred to his work, while in high school and was determined to follow in her father's footsteps. Medical school, followed by the police profession provided little time for dating and she had no interest in getting romantically involved, although as an attractive, petite blonde; in possession of a likeable personality and the only child of wealthy parents, she was being pursued by several single, young troopers. To date, those lucky enough to secure a date with her, had failed to capture her heart, or interest.

Shaking her head in a negative motion, while greeting Tom, Claire said, "Cause of death is obvious; and unfortunately, nothing much found that will aid in identifying the perpetrators."

A scowling Doc. Hartigan added, "Damned overkill! Every one of them was riddled by bullets apparently fired from some sort of machinegun. Officers Morrow and Oates are not recognizable and DNA will have to confirm their identity. I retrieved a couple of 'rounds' from Deputy Hoskin and Claire secured them for examination and analysis by your lab. My guess is they are 9-mm, and there are several types of machine guns that use that caliber. The one that comes to my mind is the Uzi, which is most notably used by the Israeli military. Tom, those damned French gold coins found in the lake have caused a killing spree. I hope your force is able to put an end to it. I was elected Coroner, 20-years ago, and for 19-years Clinton County, averaged 3 or 4 homicides per year. In the last 5 months, I have conducted seven autopsies on murder victims and it is wearing thin. I am growing old and getting called out in the middle of the night to deal with blood and gore is getting old and wearing thin. Maybe I should pack it in, and let someone younger (he nodded his head toward Claire), deal with it."

"C'mon Doc," Tom retorted, "You know you love your work, you have a good rep. and you take delight in chastising rookie cops for not handling evidence properly. What would we do without your expertise, your wit and your charm? Besides, if you retired, you would just grow bored sipping martinis, while sitting on your deck, staring out at the lake."

"Yeah, your right, and Martha (his wife) would nag me constantly about being a slob, messing up the house and getting in her way. Also have to consider losing out on invites to attend all those enjoyable state police parties and celebrations. I guess I will have to grin and bear it."

6

Tom reported back to the command post and learned from Red Whalen that no evidence or leads had yet come in. The group assembled in the squad room discussed the lack of witnesses and attributed that negative to the hour the escape occurred and dearth of residences in the immediate area of the jail. Several jail inmates, who were not targeted and were not injured, confirmed there were at least four attackers inside the jail. All were garbed in dark, military style clothing and wore dark ski masks. One inmate, John Budman, serving a 90-day sentence for Possession of Marihuana, reported that as an army veteran, he believed the attackers were ex-military or had military training. He also advised that every attacker was armed with a small machinegun.

"How and where in hell did these pukes obtain machineguns," BCI Captain Sampson voiced to the group? The Captain was a 20-year member of the force and presently supervisor of the Troop B Criminal Bureau of Investigation. He was appreciated by members under his command for recognizing that the unit supervisor in each of Troop B's stations was better equipped to supervise investigations in their area than officers, because they were completely familiar with the environment, the local law enforcement community; as well as the ethos of the residents; and therefore when responding to serious crimes, where his presence was required, he maintained a low profile. Like Tom, Sampson, was a veteran of the Marine Corps and still sported a grey crew-cut atop his lean, six-foot-four body. He was known as a tough, no-nonsense Trooper during the years he patrolled the highways and was quickly promoted to BCI Investigator. As an investigator, tireless devotion to duty began to take a toll on his marriage, and he sought relief from a bottle. When his wife threatened to leave him, he agreed to attend marriage counseling and taking the astute counselor's advice, he commenced attending AA meetings. The marriage survived, he gave up alcohol and became a teetotaler. Answering his own question, he said, "It is my guess they either purchased the guns illegally, or stole them."

"I agree Captain," Tom responded. "If you have the right contacts and big bucks required, they are available. It is reasonable to presume Bashoul has both. It certainly seems he has been able to field a large number of devoted followers to do his bidding and kill people."

As the hours ticked off the clock, virtually no information was forthcoming from the approximate 200 police officers manning road blocks and border check points.

The station driveway gradually filled with media vans, which had spent most of the early-late morning hours broadcasting from and filming the Clinton County Jail complex. They would now camp out at the Plattsburgh SP station, waiting for a break in the investigation, or another sensational incident, to occur. Captain Burrows was doing a fine job of placating the piranha, and kept them from harassing every police officer who appeared at the station, by promising hourly updates. He also assured them that if any important developments occurred, he would brief them immediately.

Burrows caused smiles to appear on the solemn faces of his fellow officers when he told them, "Men, I was eagerly looking forward to ogling Channel 5's sexy newscaster Susan James, and offering her a private session at Anthony's bistro, but was disappointed in that regard. Seems Susan is on vacation and with a 'squeeze' in Bermuda. At least that's what I was told by the little nerd from Channel 5 filling in for her. When she returns, she will be disappointed to learn she missed out on the biggest news story of the year and I am jealous and disappointed that I am not in Bermuda with her."

Forty year old Reggie Burrows had recently become divorced and commenced living the life of a playboy. Tall, possessing the dark, handsome looks of former movie actor Clark Gable, and the attractive personality of John Wayne, Reggie had little difficulty attracting women. Of course after submitting to Reggie's charm, they would be disappointed in learning that this 'Prince Charming' had no intention of re-marrying and settling down. It was known that Reggie had hit on Susan James following the murder of Stan LaPierre, and was surprised and disappointed to learn she harbored a strong dislike for police officers. Why, he did not know but he attributed her behavior to having some sort of negative police experience.

Tom grew more frustrated as the minutes and hours ticked off the clock. Pondering what to do it occurred to him to call RCMP Sergeant Scott McCormick. McCormick was most familiar with Omar Bashoul, and he might have a suggestion that would aid the investigation. He was in luck as Scott answered his phone on the first ring. Tom opened with, "Scott, I hate to be a pain in the ass, but I-we, really need your help. I am sure you are aware that Bashoul busted out of our county jail early this morning. It was accomplished by a well-planned, well-organized, military type raid, involving several attackers. Explosives were used and two sheriff's deputies and two police officers killed. So far, we don't have 'Jack Shit,' and have drawn a blank. It is reasonable to assume that Bashoul's assault team came down from Canada.

My friend, you were instrumental in facilitating our capture of Bashoul before, and I desperately need your help now."

After answering, "G-day Tom, Scott remained silent and listened as the New York State Police detective uttered his plea. When Tom concluded, he responded, "My good man, it sounds like you are up to your ears in doggy doo. Like a few million other folks – thanks to CNBC – I am aware of the mess down on your side of the border. To tell you the truth, after we nabbed Bashoul, I assumed you yanks would keep him tucked in a 6x9 for the rest of his worthless life, and moved my focus on to another 'Mutt.' I can tell you, your FBI gave me a jingle on 9/11 and asked that we cooperate in gathering Bashoul's telephone and financial records. A couple of our lads, who handle that sort of thing, gathered that info and provided it to them. Have you reached out to our friend Jason Black? Jason may have an idea or two that will put you on the trail of Bashoul."

"No, Scott. I last saw Jason at our get together on the tenth. He called me the following day to relate how the Utica paper reported Bashoul's arrest. A lot of errors in the article, and we shared a laugh over a sentence that said, 'Sources in Montreal told the Sentinel that Omar Bashoul is a respected Imam at an Islamic mosque in the city.' We chatted a bit about family and Jason advised that he and Patty were leaving on a two week Hawaiian vacation. I presume he is still enjoying himself and will wait a bit before contacting him. You might be interested in knowing that an award of $100,000 has been posted for information aiding in Bashoul's arrest. The Clinton County Sheriff's Association and Fraternal Police Federation are putting up $50,000 and the Clinton County Chamber of Commerce $50,000. The reward will be announced by media outlets today."

"Good show! I can advise that Abdul's Specialty store, remains open and a young Muslim lovely is running the show.

I am surprised that as a Muslim Imam, Abdul would leave the operation in the hands of an 'inferior' female. It is reasonable of me to guess, she is – or rather was – Abdul's main squeeze. Do you want 'us' to try wringing information from her?"

"That might be of help," Tom replied, then added "what about the Mosque he was a leader in? Can you squeeze anyone there?"

"Highly doubtful, my good man, those folks are loyal to their pastoral leader and cling together like ants on honey. We can give it a stab though, but don't get your hopes up. Oh, it just came to mind, do you remember Lisha Ishmani, the young lady that Bashoul sent to Horban, to sate Horban's sexual appetite?"

"Of course, after being raped and abused by Horban, she went to the police and you tipped me off that she was willing to cooperate. She was instrumental in us scaring the crap out of Horban, and convincing him to participate in the 'sting' that captured Bashoul."

"Well, she now totally despises Bashoul, although she remains afraid of him. I will pay her a visit to see if she can provide any information that might be helpful."

"Thanks, Scott! I know you will do your best and whatever help you can provide is greatly appreciated."

"Tom, me lad, it gives me pleasure to be of assistance to you 'Mounties' south of the border. I will be jingling you back soon."

"My best Scott, and I will keep my fingers, and toes crossed, that something turns up."

After completing his call to Scott McCormick, Tom sat at his desk pondering what more he could do to push the investigation forward. Nothing came to mind and the silence that greeted him from the adjoining squad room full of people was ominous. He took the opportunity to skim through the pile of paper in his "In" basket; realized he was not up to handling administrative work at the moment and returned the pile to the basket. He glanced at the clock on his office wall, noting it was 3 p.m. His kids would be arriving home from school. He decided to take this opportunity to surprise Liz and his kids. He entered the squad room and inquired as to whether anyone would care if he took a break and went home. His question apparently caused everyone, as frustrated as he was, to think of their families. Major O'Neill suggested, "Good idea Tom. I think we all need some respite. Other than Captain Burrows, who is stuck handling the media, let's all go home, get some rest and plan to report back here at 7 a.m. If anything pops before then, we will immediately regroup. Good afternoon men. Get some rest."

It was late afternoon when Tom arrived home. He entered the house through the front door and called out, "Honey, surprise, I am home!"

Liz was surprised when Tom arrived home so early, on a day that the media was proclaiming as the day the most shocking criminal event in the history of the North Country occurred. She happened to observe Tom drive into the driveway and was immediately concerned as to why he was home so early; she wondered if he was sick. When he threw open the front door announcing his arrival, in a healthy sounding voice, her concern evaporated.

She met him in the front hallway and rushed into his arms. They exchanged a passionate kiss, then still clinging together, studied each other's face. For a moment, neither spoke, just appreciating the intimacy of the moment. Then they drew together, exchanged a passionate kiss, after which, Tom broke the silence, "Where's all of our rug rats?"

Smiling, Liz explained, "Mary and Susan are at cheerleading practice. Jeremy is in football practice and Bobby is going to catch the late bus with them, as he is studying for a Math test. Joe is next door at Bart and Harriet's, playing with Rascal, their toy poodle."

"Great! That means you can sit with me for a bit and I will bring you up to date as to what happened. First, let me 'fix' some medicine (Martinis), and then we'll go out on the deck, where the beauty and peace of 'our' lake will ease the burden of my news."

Tom then entered the kitchen and prepared a shaker of vodka Martini's, 'shaken not stirred,' filled two glasses and garnished Liz's drink with two lime peels. He opted for two large Spanish olives in his. He presented Liz her drink and they went out onto the magnificent 12' x 40' deck, attached to the rear of their home, overlooking beautiful Lake Champlain.

For several minutes Tom and Liz stood in silence enjoying a vista that some visitors had referred to as paradise. Finally, Tom broke the silence and commenced relating the details of Bashoul's escape, minimizing the gory details. However, desirous of having Liz offer prayers and assistance to the families of the slain officers, he explained that they died a hero's death and death came quickly. Liz advised that she would accompany Tom to each man's funeral and would personally reach out to the widow's and offer them assistance.

Having imparted his message, Tom sat in silence studying the lake. The obelisk on Crab Island, one mile off shore, stood tall and proud in the glow of sunlight, and it always caused Tom to reflect on its historic meaning. Seemingly incredible, during the naval battle on Plattsburgh Bay, during the War of 1812, Crab Island became a hospital, where wounded and deceased from both sides were taken for treatment of their injuries, or burial. Historically, approximately 50 sailors and marines killed in the engagement, were buried together on the small island. A hundred years later a monument was erected on the island to pay honor and tribute to those who were buried there. Across the lake, the Green

Mountains of Vermont presented a magnificent backdrop to the artistry and serenity of the lake. Pleasure boats and fishing boats skimmed the lake's surface. Looking to the north, they studied the Cumberland to Grand Isle ferries crossing the lake. Looking to the south, the north end of Valcour Island appeared serene and green. As Tom studied the island he reflected on the events that had disrupted his formerly idyllic life. *Oh, Jack and Stan, why did you have to find 'Champ's cave?* The discovery of the cave, home of 'Champ' and containing the golden treasure, was responsible for so much death and destruction. The discovery of that damned cave had disrupted his formerly idyllic life and introduced that demon Bashoul. He sighed during this reflection and muttered loud enough for Liz to hear, "That damned gold! Surely a curse is associated with it. Life was so much easier for all of us before the glitter of gold and dreams of wealth, polluted minds and triggered greed. Death, destruction and misery have been the result."

"I heard you Tom," Liz whispered, "but apparently it was destined that Jack and Stan discover that treasure. Also, consider how awesome it is, that at the same time they discovered that 'Champ' is real, and not just a myth or legend. It is awesome that one of God's creations that lived on earth before 'He' created man, is still alive and living – hopefully in peace – in our lake. And, recall the four times we saw 'Champ' on the lake. When you told Captain Pabst of our sighting, he scoffed and said 'Champ' was a myth and what we had observed was simply an anomaly in the lake. We haven't seen Frank lately, but I would guess the discovery that 'Champ' is real astounds and amazes him. He is now able to awe passengers on his *Juniper* lake cruise boat with tales about a sea monster, and will have them hanging over the rail looking for 'Champ'."

"We cannot turn back the clock Tom! Let's just give thanks to God, for permitting us to enjoy the majesty and beauty of this lake. Let us also thank 'Him' for permitting us the love we have for each other and for giving us five wonderful children."

Hearing the school bus stopping in front of the house, Tom responded, "Thank you for opening my eyes and cooling my overheated brain, another reason I love you so much. Let's go greet our kids."

That evening, Tom enjoyed participation in a sit down dinner with family. Helen and Jack Weston joined in savoring the pork roast that Liz cooked to perfection. Dinner conversation – of course – focused on the events of the previous day. Not wanting to cause undo concern, though in truth he was concerned, Tom mentioned to his Aunt and Jack, that, 'just as a precaution' they were being assigned state police security until Bashoul was apprehended. He also showed them an object in the form of a medallion attached to a neck chain. The object was in truth a transponder that would send out an electronic signal if a tiny button on the rear were pressed. He instructed that they were to wear this necklace at all times and – "God forbid," in the event of an emergency, they were to press the button.

After savoring a slice of delicious, homemade, apple pie, Tom and Jack enjoyed an after dinner cordial on the deck, while the Weston children worked on assigned homework and Liz and Helen were busy chatting, clearing the dinner table and loading a dishwasher.

Jack echoed Tom's earlier day reflection, "Uncle Tom, I regret having stumbled upon 'the cave.' If we hadn't found the lost French gold coins, my dearest friend, would now be seated beside us on your deck. My life turned to hell after the excitement of that day. Stan and I were so elated, and we dreamed of wealth and fame. We had no inkling that our discovery would result in so much misery, death and destruction."

"Jack, stop blaming yourself for failing to perceive what might result from you finding the gold. As you know, many divers, including myself, searched for the treasure and if I had been the one to find it, the same result would probably have occurred. Let's change the subject. Helen told me, that yesterday you were accepted for employment in the Sheriff's Department. That is wonderful news, and a little bird told me that after you are sworn in, a wedding is taking place. Kathleen has been patient and loving for a long time. She will be a wonderful wife. Congratulations!"

Jack's voice was full of emotion as he extended his right hand and responded, "Uncle Tom, if not for you, I would not be here and I would not be alive!"

Tom clasped his nephew's hand in his and drew him into an embrace. "Hey, you big lug, we are family and I love you! I did not save you Jack. Actually, God must have heard me praying and he decided you've got a lot of life yet to live."

After releasing each other, both removed a handkerchief from a pocket and dabbed at their eyes.

They entered the house and as he entered, Jack gave Liz a hug and a smile, as he stated, "You served a delicious meal. I am sure that Uncle Tom has to be at work early in the morning, so mom and I will bid you adieu. Thank you for a wonderful evening."

Hugs were exchanged, then, Helen and Jack were out the door. After they departed, Tom gathered Liz in his arms, gazed into her eyes and whispered, "You were an excellent hostess and served a delicious meal topped off by scrumptious apple pie. You, my sweet, have many talents including one that at the present time has me feeling very amorous."

"Well, lover boy, put your passion on hold for a bit. "We've got to get the kids into bed first and assure they are asleep."

Joe was playing a game on the living room floor. His older siblings were in the family room hopefully working on homework rather than watching television.

"Hey guys," Tom called, "mom and dad are very tired and I've got a big day tomorrow, how about giving old Dad a hug, and then heading off to bed. You can dream about the trip we are going to take to Disney World, when this mess I am working on is cleared up."

Hugs, accompanied by, "I love you," were exchanged and twenty minutes later Liz was tucking in and planting a kiss on every child. Tom was already in bed waiting for Liz to join him. His anticipation of passion pushed Bashoul and police work out of his mind. Since Stan's murder, the attempt to murder Jack, and all of the death attributed to Omar Bashoul, Tom's long work hours, accompanied by stress, had crimped his performance in bed. Of late, their love-making had become a 'slam-bam-thank you-ma'am' situation. Afterwards, Tom was quickly snoring; whereas, having been denied fulfillment, Liz lay awake praying that the nightmare that was impacting their lives would soon end. She reflected on all the times their lovemaking had been a symphony of passion, with an overture of slow exploration, then rising in tempo and ending in a breathtaking crescendo finale. Five beautiful children had resulted from those symphonies. As the man she loved so dearly, was presently at peace, this night, they would perform another symphony. After a mutual explosive finale, contented and at peace, Liz kept one hand gently touching her husband's face and smiled, as she heard Tom snoring.

The Weston house phone and Tom's cell phone remained silent the rest of the night. Tom awakened to the delicious aroma of cooking bacon. He jumped out of bed, took a quick shower, whistling a tune as hot water ran over his body. After drying, he hurriedly dressed, ran a comb through his still blonde, but thinning hair, then dashed downstairs. Liz, still clad in a lacy nightgown and terry robe, was frying bacon and eggs while conversing with Mary, Susan, Jeremy, Bobby and Joe, who were wolfing down cereal and muffins slathered with PBJ. She had heard her husband whistling and she was elated that he was feeling happy. Tom, pecked Liz on the cheek, plopped down in his seat at the dining room table and snatched up the Plattsburgh Press-Republican paper, which Liz had placed on the table. Liz, smiled as she studied him and silently prayed, "Dear Jesus, please watch over and protect my husband."

"Hey Dad," Jeremy asked, "Are you mentioned in today's paper."

Giving his son a smile, Tom replied, "No. Thank God, not today. Sadly, the news deals with the attack on the County jail, Bashoul's escape and the murder of four fine police officers.

Some of the reported details are not accurate, but what else is new. The article sort of portrays Omar Bashoul, or Abdul Markesh, whoever he is, as some sort of genius who continues to outsmart police at every turn. I am pleased to see that they give hero status to Hughes, Oates, Morrow and Hoskin, and describe the impact of their loss on their families."

Tom arrived at the Plattsburgh station at 7:15 a.m. and upon exiting his car was immediately besieged by members of the media. He was deluged by questions relating to the progress of the investigation and if the arrest of Bashoul was imminent. Holding both hands up with palms facing outward to fend off the bombardment of questions, he stated, "Ladies and gentlemen, I have nothing new to report at this time. Captain Burrows will be holding a press briefing at 9 a.m." His response was met by an incoherent grumbling from tired reporters, each of whom was hopeful of learning of Bashoul's arrest, so they could bid adieu to the North Country. Plattsburgh had proved to be a quiet boring city to those accustomed to the hustle and bustle of the major metropolitan cities where their headquarters were located. Tom ignored the grumbling and shouted questions went unanswered, as he entered the station. Upon entering he was greeted by Zone Sergeant Melanie Gibbs, who had been studying the group of media people gathered outside.

Melanie chuckled as Tom entered and greeted, "Good morning Tom. I noticed you managed to make your way unscathed through the school of 'piranha' thirsting for blood."

Displaying a scowl, Tom responded, "Yeah and they already have my day off to a bad start. How are you Mel?"

Melanie smiled as she responded, "Taking one day at a time Tom and searching for Prince Charming." Recently divorced and struggling to keep her rebellious teenage son out of jail, the 42- year old, prematurely gray, slightly overweight sergeant; a 14 year member of the state police, was appreciated as a low-key supervisor, who was respected by those who knew and worked with her. Most co-workers were of the opinion that Melanie's son was angry over the breakup of his parent's marriage and was releasing his anger by smoking marihuana, skipping school and hanging out with unsavory characters. The fact that his father was an alcoholic and had basically abandoned him contributed to his anger.

"Hang tough Mel! Life is bound to improve soon and your prince will appear. Do you have any good news that will get my day started off with a smile rather than a scowl?"

"Nope, zone's been quiet all night and I quelled the piranha's appetites by informing them that the restaurant and bar at Plattsburgh's 'City Beach Marina,' served excellent food and was open until 3 a.m. I believe most decided to check it out."

"One of my favorite summer haunts," Tom responded, "Get some sleep Mel, and if I run across any good Prince Charming prospects today, I will let you know."

Tom was surprised to find Red Whalen, looking fresh and smelling of liberally applied after-shave, already seated at his desk in the BCI squad room. He was equally surprised that Red was the sole occupant of the room. Red looked up from the crossword puzzle he was working on in the morning newspaper and greeted, "Good morning Boss! What is a goose called in Hawaii?"

Tom chuckled and responded, "Hey Red! You are bright and chipper this morning. Do you have any good news for me?"

"Nope, I came in early to review my notes from yesterday. Not much to review. I know you are a smart dude and a devotee of crossword puzzles, boss. As you didn't respond to my question, am I to presume you don't know the answer."

Giving Red a mischievous smile, Tom replied, "That's an easy one Red. The answer is 'Nene.' Ask me a hard one?"

"What is a four letter word for the language of Pakistan?"

"Another easy one Red try, 'Urdu.'" Tom chuckled and added, "You are obviously trying to solve the puzzle in the Plattsburgh-Press Republican and not the New York Times."

"You are a twit, Boss. Are you insulting my intelligence?"

"No way, Red, why do you think I always select you to be case scribe for our difficult cases?" Answering his own question, he added, "I know you are intelligent and a good writer."

"I suppose I should say that I appreciate that; however, you know boss, I would prefer being involved in the front lines."

Tom chuckled again and responded, "Case scribe is a very important function Red, and I know I can count on you to keep all of the information flowing in from various sources in proper and intelligent order. Consider yourself in the front lines, because trying to decipher scrawling and gibberish from a variety of personalities and then making it intelligible for supervisors to read and digest has got to be stressful. Believe me, every supervisor takes notice and appreciates your report writing expertise."

"Thank you Boss! Oh, I did receive a call from Chief Reeves. Seems Morrow and Oates were both Catholic, and parishioners at Saint John's Catholic church. Their families have decided to hold a dual funeral mass, at St. John's on Wednesday, at 1 p.m. I took the liberty to call Captain Storch (Zone Commander), and he is initiating a request with the TC (Troop Commander) for maximum police attendance. Following the funeral mass, Morrow is going to be buried in Saint Augustine cemetery in Peru. The Oates family opted for cremation. That's all the information I have. Haven't heard when services are going to be held for Hughes and Hoskins. You want me to call Sheriff Benson?"

"Thanks for the info. Red, Liz and I will – of course – attend the funerals and pay tribute. It would be a nice gesture if every member of our unit was there." He added, "You don't have to call the Sheriff because I am certain he will be contacting us."

"Well, you can count on me attending, and I would guess the rest of 'the guys' will go."

"Are the road blocks still being manned?"

"Yeah, but according to Zone Commander Storch, only till noon today."

"So, Red, what good news do you have to report?"

Smiling, Red responded, "The sun is shining, and according to the Plattsburgh Press-Republican, the stock market is up."

"Yeah, and Bashoul is thumbing his nose at us."

7

The following Wednesday morning, Tom donned the black suit, referred to as his 'wedding and funeral suit' and Liz selected a mauve colored tie to wear with his white dress shirt. She opted to wear a black knee length dress, black medium heel shoes and her only jewelry would be a strand of imitation pearls.

Tom stared at his wife as she was stretching nylons on her legs and whistled. "Babe, when I see you putting on nylons, it gets me very excited. I don't know how you manage to maintain such an exquisite body, but whatever, it is greatly appreciated."

Liz responded with a scowl, "Tom Weston, I am dressing for a very solemn, depressing occasion. Start acting professional! Get your mind off sex and concentrate on where we are going and the purpose of our going there!"

Giving his wife a sheepish look in return, Tom apologized, "Sorry Honey, but you are beautiful and you do turn me on."

"Well turn off that switch lover boy, and tune in to the reality of the day."

Liz was not pleased with the news that Tom had been asked to join the ranks of police officers that would gather outside the church. Although St. John's Catholic Church was fairly large, in comparison to many churches, it was anticipated there would not be enough seating for the horde of police officers that would be attending. Tom had indicated that seating priority was first for family and immediate friends.

He told his wife, "As you are considered a friend of both families, you will be ushered to a seat. If you can save room for your large husband, I will sneak in and join you for Mass. Just before the conclusion of services, I will leave you and rejoin my workmates in the ranks outside the church. The funeral cortege going to the cemetery will be long and Troopers have been assigned at every intersection along the way to halt traffic and facilitate the flow of the funeral procession. Liz, Officers Oates and Morrow, are getting a hero's send-off – which they were – and all the 'bigwigs' in state and local government will be in attendance. I expect that the road through the cemetery will not be able to accommodate all the vehicles. Many folks intending on going to the cemetery, will be forced to park at a distance. Wisely, Major O'Neill considered that possibility and has assigned troopers to operate golf carts to pick up those folks parked at a distance and bring them to the gravesite. Bluff Point Golf Club is providing the golf carts. Are you planning on going to the cemetery?"

"No, Tom. I will be joining a group of approximately 50 women, serving all you hungry men, in Saint Augustine's Social Hall, following the service. I agreed to bake apple pies and cookies, which are ready and waiting. I will go home from St. John's pick up my baked goods and then meet you later at St. Augustine's in Peru. I expect you will be returning to work after the funerals, so I plan, after cleaning up at St. Augustine's to spend some time with Ellen Morrow and Susan Oates, to give them encouragement. I know, I would be devastated if something happened to take you from me, and I would be seeking a shoulder to cry on. Thank goodness Ellen and Susan have strong, loving families to aid them. I will probably arrive home at around seven this evening, and though I won't count on it, hope you are home."

"Who is going to greet our kids when they arrive home from school, and feed them supper?"

"I prepared a tuna casserole for them. This morning I instructed Mary to heat the casserole up and dish it out to her siblings. I also left a fresh apple pie on the counter and they can have vanilla ice cream with pie for dessert."

"What about Bobby?"

"Bart and Harriett (next door neighbors), are watching Bobby. Tom, if you paid more attention to family, you would already know these things."

"Yeah, I know, I'm always focused on arresting bad guys, or making love to my beautiful wife."

Shaking her head while displaying a look of disgust, Liz, responded, "Tom Weston, you are incorrigible!"

"Incorrigibly in love with you my beautiful sweet wife!" He gathered her in his arms, they exchanged a quick kiss and then Tom headed for the door. "See you at church love!"

Funeral details, accompanied by many photos, filled the front page of the Thursday edition of the Plattsburgh Press-Republican. It was reported that approximately 1000 police, fire and emergency responders, from all over the United States and Canada, attended to pay their respect to the fallen heroes. Monsignor Michael Hulihan, presided at the funeral Mass, assisted by priests, from several Catholic churches. In his homily, Monsignor Hulihan proclaimed that both officers had not died in vain, as they were rushing to aid fellow officers, fellow man, and died as heroes; their souls immediately greeted by Jesus. Eulogies were offered by New York Governor Bickford Roberts, and Plattsburgh Police Chief Harold Reeves. It was also reported that the City of Plattsburgh was virtually at a standstill during the funeral services; however, citizens, for the most part were understanding and cooperative. It was also pointed out that the funeral procession stretched from the City of Plattsburgh to the Hamlet of Peru, which made it the longest funeral procession in the history of Clinton County. The ceremony at the cemetery was brief; however, very emotional and heart wrenching as the honor guard presented a folded ensign to Morrow's widow, while the strains of Amazing Grace played by an unseen bagpiper echoed across the hillside. The entire Plattsburgh BCI squad had attended the funerals and they all stood together in solemn silence throughout the graveside services. As professionals accustomed to dealing with death, they managed to hold their emotions in check.

However, when the skirl of an unseen bagpiper commenced playing Amazing Grace, tears commenced wetting the faces of most in attendance. Tom and Red reached for handkerchiefs, and Patty produced tissue to wipe away the flow of tears. Ed, Enrico and Vic were able to remain dry eyed, only because angry emotion overwhelmed sad emotion.

Wednesday had been a traumatic day and proved to be another frustrating day as no new information or evidence was reported.

The following day, it was time to do it all over again. Tom donned his 'wedding-funeral suit again in preparation to attend the 10 a.m. funeral of Sheriff's Sergeant Hughes, with service to be held at The First Baptist Church in Plattsburgh, followed by burial in Riverside Cemetery, also in Plattsburgh. Sergeant Hughes and his family attended the church and their pastor, the Reverend Claude Williams, presided at the funeral. As in the send off for the two Plattsburgh police officers, a record crowd of police, fire, emergency personnel, as well as City and County residents attended. Though probably 60-years old, Rev. Williams; having a handsome face topped by thick, wavy, dark hair, appeared much younger. The Rev. was noted as an inspiring speaker and his sermon covered many aspects of Sheriff Hughes life, including Hughes work with troubled youngsters who had run afoul of the law. As a matter of interest, Hughes and his wife had raised ten troubled foster children and all ten were now good students, participating in youth groups. "Ted Hughes loved his wife, his children, his community; and being a police officer. He will be sorely missed by all who knew him; however, they must take solace and feel blessed by God, for having known a soldier of God, who dedicated himself to helping others. Sheriff's Sergeant Theodore Hughes is now at peace and if you, my dear friends, follow his example in life, you will join him in Heaven."

Governor Roberts delivered a brief eulogy, in which he praised Hughes for being a well-liked police professional; a man who loved his work, loved his family and who died a hero.

Sheriff Benson paid honor by relating many of Sergeant Hughes accomplishments as a member of the Clinton County Sheriff's Department, and that he would be sorely missed by friends and co-workers.

As Riverside Cemetery was in the City of Plattsburgh, once again, the city was basically at a stand-still throughout the late morning and early afternoon. Similar to the graveside closing ceremony of the previous day, tears flowed freely as the chilling strains of a bagpipe played Amazing Grace while the honor guard presented a folded ensign to Hughes widow.

The funeral for Deputy Morrow the following day was a more subdued affair. The Morrow family was not aligned with any particular religious affiliation and although Sheriff Mark Benson, during, his visit to the Morrow home following the shooting, indicated that the County would provide an elegant funeral, Debbie Morrow, the Deputy's wife, opted for a service at the funeral home. Fifty-four year old Mark Benson was elected Sheriff of Clinton County in 1998, after serving first as a deputy sheriff and was appointed as second in command of the Clinton

County Sheriff's Department by popular Sheriff Will Waters. When Waters announced he was retiring due to health issues, he recommended Under Sheriff Benson replace him. The popular Sheriff's endorsement made it a 'shoe in' for Benson and he ran unopposed for the position. Mark Benson was a gregarious, likeable Andy Griffith look-alike, who was well-respected by all who knew him.

Approximately 700 police, fire and emergency services personnel, stood in ranks in the funeral home parking lot, while Sheriff Benson – delivered a brief eulogy, praising the young deputy for serving the people of Clinton County to the best that could be expected of any law enforcement officer. He added, "Doug possessed an endearing smile that warmed everyone he came in contact with. His smile, likeable personality and dedication to duty will be missed. Every member of the Clinton County Sheriff's Department was family and Doug's nuclear family can count on assistance from his professional family."

The family indicated that they welcomed any and all dignitaries to attend the service, but opting for brevity, requested no eulogies from those in attendance.

At the conclusion of the service, the ranks of those gathered outside, filed one-by-one into the funeral parlor and paid their last respects. During this period brevity was lost, and as many of the mourners stopped briefly before the closed casket, they paused to offer brief prayer. Those who knew Morrow, personally, briefly embraced his widow and offered their support.

There was no funeral cortege as the family opted for cremation.

Attending funerals, although necessary, but never enjoyable, had been tiring and taken a toll on the Weston's. Tom was physically and emotionally tired, and at each of the funerals he had silently prayed that the death and destruction associated with

Omar Mohammed Bashoul, was at an end, though he was not optimistic that it was. Liz was physically and emotionally drained from worry about her husband and family and all of the work in preparing food and serving hundreds of people. She had also asked each of the widows to feel free to call on her for physical and/or emotional assistance.

8

Former Canadian Minister of Justice Angus Horban, admired himself in his massive bathroom mirror. At 62-years of age, he kept muscular and trim, via twice daily workouts involving aerobics and weights. Standing 6 feet 5 inches, he was physically impressive; however, his head seemed too small for his physique and a narrow, pocked marked face, caused by an early age case of chicken pox detracted from his appearance, as did the too dark toupee that covered a bald pate. Rather than studying his face, he flexed his arms in the mirror and displayed a contented smile. While admiring his physique, he reflected on the events of the past month, and such reflection changed an egotistical smile into a scowl. *I should never have gotten involved with that damned Bashoul. When Boosha (Canadian Minister of Health) introduced me to Bashoul, I never perceived the possibility that Bashoul was connected with Islamic terrorists and no one would ever learn that he was sending young lovelies to me. The bastard cost me my position in the Ministry and tarnished my reputation. I am fortunate to have been allowed to quietly resign and resume a normal life. After Bashoul was arrested, I presumed I would never have to concern myself with him again. How was I to perceive that the clumsy American system of justice would fail to take measures that ensured he would not escape from their jail and I have to assume that my life is now in danger, thank the Good Lord I have the financial means to hire bodyguards.*

It was a lovely September day and Angus planned to meet Minister Boosha for lunch, upon conclusion of his visit to Gold's gym for a workout. Subsequent to learning of Bashoul's escape, he hired two retired police officers who presented credentials indicating expertise in karate and the use of firearms. The two men alternated 12-hour security shifts, ensuring that one of them was with Horban at all times. The one going by the name, Jacques Fenlau, was presently standing outside his employer's bedroom door waiting for the day to begin. Horban met him in the hallway and they proceeded downstairs. Horban did not immediately exit his home, instead standing impatiently inside the front door, waiting for Fenlau to inform him it was safe to come outside. Horban was not a patient man and did not appreciate being kept waiting. He paced about in the foyer of his palatial home, periodically looking at his watch and cussing under his breath. Finally, a black limousine drove through the front gate and stopped in the inner circle of the drive that fronted the residence. Fenlau was pleased to note that the limo driver knew the electronic gate security code provided to the manager of the limo service. The manager had been instructed not to provide this code to anyone else who might ask for it.

After stopping, the driver exited the vehicle and followed instructions to step away from the vehicle. Then Fenlau patted down the uniform clad driver and examined the inside of the vehicle. Nothing was observed that garnered suspicion, so he spoke into the lapel microphone he was wearing and Horban came outside.

The short, plump, driver had a friendly face and displayed a friendly demeanor while being ordered about and treated impolitely by Horban's security guard. When Horban appeared, he held open the passenger compartment door, while his passengers entered the vehicle. Horban entered the car first and the burly, muscular security guard then got in and sat beside his employer.

Angus eyed the limo driver for a brief moment before getting in the vehicle, and stated, "I don't recognize you. Where is Jacques?"

Displaying a smile, the driver responded, "Jacques is not feeling well today. I am Nolle, Sir, and it is my pleasure to serve you today."

After Horban and Fenlau were seated, the limo driver reached inside the driver's compartment and pressed a button that locked the rear doors, preventing them from being opened. Then he removed an object from his pocket and walked away from the vehicle. As he did, Fenlau drew his weapon, and shot out the glass of the passenger compartment. This action came too late, as the limo driver pushed the button on the device he was holding. In the explosion that followed, former Minister of Justice Angus Horban and his bodyguard were immediately reduced to body parts and the limousine was reduced to a pile of rubble.

The body of Jacques Monteque, Horban's regular limo driver, was subsequently found by police in the bathtub of his apartment. Post mortem examination would reveal he had been garroted and his body bore no additional signs of torture or trauma.

9

Subsequent to learning of the attack on 9/11, Tom volunteered to be part of the state police contingent that was being sent to New York City to assist the New York Police Department. Liz was thankful that her husband's request was denied. Troop Commander O'Neill informed Tom that he was needed in Plattsburgh to supervise and coordinate efforts to apprehend Omar Bashoul. He also was needed to supervise the protection of his nephew and any other potential witnesses against Bashoul.

Sergeant Scott McCormick, had called Tom to report the assassination of Angus Horban, and Tom having tuned in to Chanel 5 news reports, was aware of Horban's death. Scott advised that a special unit of Royal Canadian Mounted Police, and Quebec Provincial Police, had been formed to investigate Horban's death and that of his bodyguard. As part of this investigation, they planned to investigate Bashoul's past and attempt to locate any associates.

Scott and Tom communicated regularly by phone, and in a call, shortly after Bashoul's escape from the Clinton County jail, Scott had reported, "Mate, it will probably be of no surprise to learn Bashoul was regularly communicating with Mohamed Atta, the baddie Muslim who flew the plane into your World Trade Center. So, it appears obvious that Bashoul had a hand in the carnage of September 11th. I have already provided this info to

your esteemed FBI, and they asked whether our scan of Bashoul's telephone records revealed any calls to mid-eastern countries. We didn't find any calls; however, his banking records reveal he was receiving monthly transfers of money from a Saudi, using the name 'Taqiyah.' If you are up-to-date on the Arabic language and some of the idioms associated, 'Taqiyah' is a term associated with pretense. Taqiyah allows a devout Muslim to pretend to be your best buddy, while in truth he is planning to cut your throat."

"Most interesting Scott, were you able to identify the true identity of the money source?"

"My good man, our intelligence gurus are very good at what they do. They dug deep and learned Abdul had buddied up with a Saudi, while both were attending the same university. That chap goes by the name of Osama Bin Laden. Seems Bin Laden, is one of 'skate-y-eight' children of a wealthy Saudi big shot, and he is not fond of you yanks. I provided all of this info to our friend, Ray Forrest (FBI SA), who told me that the FBI was focusing on Bin Laden, as the 'probable' baddie, leading, and financing the 'nut job' Islamic suicide mission.

"Scott, you are truly a fountain of information and a magnificent detective. I could use you down here, but you are extremely valuable right where you are. We presently have a task force dedicated to locating and apprehending Bashoul. He is one clever, slippery bastard, and so far has covered his tracks well. However, I am confident his super-sized ego will eventually cause him to slip up. When that happens, I hope he resists arrest and is dispatched to his paradise, which is obviously Hell.

While I've got you on the phone, curious as to Forrest demeanor when you were talking with him?"

"He was most cordial Tom," Scott replied, "why do you ask

"Well, I called him on September 11th, soon after the jihad attacks and suggested the FBI place Ali Mahoud – you mi

remember him – in our jail, in an attempt to gain Abdul's trust and hopefully get him to incriminate himself and the whole jihadist operation. Forrest told me that he would run my idea by his supervisor. In subsequent conversation with him, a couple of days later, he was cool and informed me that the terrorist attack was in essence an act of war and resolving the crimes were the sole responsibility of the FBI. He suggested that we focus our investigation concerning Bashoul on state crimes he is responsible for, and disregard the plane terrorist attacks. On conclusion of our conversation, it seemed obvious that the FBI is not going to be sharing much information with us."

"Interesting," Scott replied. "Forrest was cordial enough during our conversation, but in retrospect, he was looking for our assistance, and he didn't offer any information concerning information the FBI had developed. Perhaps there is a massaging of egos going on down there and your feds don't want you state boys messing up their game plan and stealing their thunder."

"Actually Scott, I believe the blame can be placed at the feet of our conflicted court systems. I have worked a couple of kidnap cases with the FBI and the investigative rules they must abide by come in direct conflict with ours. You see, when the "Feebs' develop a suspect and want to make an arrest they are required to present their investigative findings to a federal prosecutor who authorizes issuance of a warrant. Our New York State Supreme Court decided that if an arrest warrant is obtained from a magistrate, the arrested subject's Miranda Rights are already invoked and the accused is automatically entitled to representation by an attorney. That makes it virtually impossible to obtain a confession. We prefer to make a summary arrest, read the subject their Miranda Rights and then try to engage them in conversation that will ultimately lead to an admission of guilt. Of course in this situation, I could be wrong that this is the reason

the FBI wants us to keep out of 'their' investigation. Following the attack, our President declared the jihadist attack was "an act of war." In all likelihood the Director of the FBI, issued the order that his agents were to keep all information concerning their investigation – in house. So, probably my astute friend, you are right. They just don't want us messing up their game plan."

"Well, Tom, we don't have our noses in the air, and we have a mutual interest in putting Bashoul where he belongs, either behind bars or better yet, in Hades. You can rely on us to keep you posted on any developments that might aid in capturing that demon and I am confident we can rely on your complete cooperation."

"Absolutely," Tom replied, adding, "Take care and hang tough Scott."

"You too, Mate!"

After concluding his conversation with Scott McCormick, Tom decided to call SA Ray Forrest at the Albany FBI office. Ray was cordial, when he answered his phone and they exchanged pleasantries. Tom then related that he was calling because of the information he had received from Scott, concerning Bashoul's connection to Bin Laden and how it appeared that Bashoul played a role in the jihadist terrorist attacks. "It is water over the dam now Ray, but I wish we had transferred Bashoul to a more secure facility, immediately after the attacks. Neither myself, nor my superiors gave any thought to the possibility that Bashoul would escape jail. That omission resulted in the murder of four police officers. We presently are engaged in an all out effort to apprehend Bashoul, but have a dearth of evidence and virtually no witnesses. You and Agent Watkins were very helpful during the investigation to solve the murder of Stan LaPierre. Do you plan to come up and assist in our effort to capture Bashoul? Also, has your investigation thus far developed any information that you are at liberty to share with me?"

"Sorry Tom, our supervisor is sending us down to New York City to participate in the gathering of evidence and interview of hundreds of witnesses who were fortunate to only be injured and not killed in the attack on the twin towers."

"Ray, what information can you share with me about this Osama Bin Laden character?"

"Sorry Tom," Ray responded. "I have been directed not to provide any information concerning Bin Laden, to anyone. That includes other police agencies and officers."

Trying not to sound agitated, Tom replied, "But it is now obvious that Omar Bashoul had some involvement in some fashion in the terrorist attacks and is connected to this Osama Bin Laden. We presently are conducting an all out manhunt to find and arrest Bashoul, for multiple counts of murder. It would seem logical that our agencies work together and after Bashoul is apprehended, he would be charged with federal, as well as state crimes."

"As I said Tom, our supervisor ordered us to stay focused on the federal crimes that were committed. I mentioned to him that the state police are after Bashoul and would be an excellent ally in our goal of identifying all involved in the jihadist plot. He emphasized that we were not to partner with other police agencies and that the Director of the FBI would request that the Superintendent of State Police have his agency assume the role of support, performing only those functions we assign to them."

Tom tried to calm down by silently counting to ten but only got as far as five. "Ray, if that is the direction the FBI is taking; your supervisor and your Director have their heads up their ass! Omar was arrested by 'us' on a murder charge, and he escaped from our local jail, murdering two sheriff's deputies and two police officers during that escape. We have no intention of abandoning pursuit of Bashoul, and if the FBI refuses to cooperate with us, then we will not share Intel with them. Give your boss that message and if he isn't pleased, he can call Major O'Neill, whom I will be calling as soon as we conclude this call. Ray, I know you are doing what you have been ordered to do and I hold no ill feelings toward you personally."

Not desirous of an answer and not waiting for one, he ended the call.

As stated, Tom immediately called Troop B Commander, Major O'Neill and filled him in on his conversation with SA Forrest.

Forty-eight year old Chris O'Neill had commanded Troop B for two years and having entered the state police at 22-years of age, he was eligible for retirement. Uniquely, O'Neill had served, first as Trooper, Investigator, Sergeant, Lieutenant and Captain in four of the state's ten troops. He had the reputation as a tough, no nonsense supervisor; however, most members of the New York State police who had worked with or for him, considered him easy going and possessing a warm-friendly personality. O'Neill was tall, slender and facially - he was often described – as a Tom Selleck look alike. Chris had joined the state police directly from college and had never served in the military; however, he insisted that all uniform members of his command be in clean and proper uniform so as to present a good public image. Major O'Neill's wife was Kirsten, and they resided in Lake Placid. They had two teenage children – a 17 year old son and 18 year old daughter. The O'Neill family, were avid skiers and during the winter spent a lot of time on the ski slopes at Whiteface Mountain.

"Screw the 'Feebs'" was his immediate response, followed by, "typical FBI arrogance and elitism. When crimes of major importance occur, they want total control and demand total allegiance from other police agencies. Tom, this inhuman Bashoul character, is responsible for numerous crimes, so you have my authority and support to use whatever means necessary to capture him. If we get him first, the feds will have to stand in line. That is with the caveat, unless the Superintendent directs otherwise. I know Superintendent Grayson well. He is old school Trooper and feels the same way about the FBI, so I don't think he will cave. Tom, I know you and every member of this troop will work tirelessly to apprehend Bashoul. Please spread the word that I don't want anyone to become exhausted and sick. Bashoul will make a mistake and we will get him."

"Thank you Major! I anticipated that would be your response."

10

Abdul was pleased to learn that the traitor Angus Horban, had met his untimely demise. His loyal assassin had executed Bashoul's plan perfectly. He rewarded Kalil Boosha by adding a bonus to the amount previously agreed upon. Now there were only a couple more details to take care of before he clandestinely departed the despised United States of America and travelled to Pakistan, where he would be reunited with Osama Bin Laden.

He was also quite pleased and proud of himself for having devised a flawless escape plan. His only regret was being cooped up in a cabin, in the remote woods of New Hampshire. He spent a great part of his long, boring day praying to Allah, and devising a plan that would kill an even greater number of American infidels. He was considering poisoning America's water reservoirs, knocking out America's electric grid system or devising a way to totally freeze the American government computer system. Accomplishing that would also neuter America's military as virtually all weapons systems were controlled by computers. In his diabolical mind that would be the best option; however, it was extremely difficult to devise a plan that would only cripple Western hemisphere computers and not infect computers world-wide. In any event, he was looking forward to collaborating with Osama and together, they would conceive a grand plan that would force the infidels to surrender to Islam.

11

Another day passed and in addition to the news received from Scott McCormick, the only piece of new evidence was positive identification that the bullets that killed the police officers were 9mm and the weapons that fired them were either Uzi or MP3. ATF was working hard to identify the source of the machine guns; however, as investigators were not even sure of the nationality of the killers, so far they had struck out.

On an additional frustrating note, Tom had no idea how the FBI were progressing with their investigation, because they were not sharing any information with the state police. He was concerned that if the 'Feebs' were looking for Bashoul, by not working with the state police any information or evidence that they gathered might be withheld from the state police. The conflict between the two agencies added to the complexity of the investigation.

After conversing with McCormick, Tom decided he needed a stiff drink and temporary escape from stress. He called Liz, informed her he was on the way home and asked if she would have a Martini ready for him when he arrived.

That morning when her husband left for work, Liz was not optimistic that she would see him again until exhaustion eventually forced him home. Therefore, she was elated that he would be spending the evening with her and their children. The shaker containing Smirnoff Vodka, with just a touch of dry Vermouth, was waiting in the fridge when her husband walked in the door. She greeted him with a hug, then, fetched the shaker, two Martini glasses and they went out on the deck to let the beauty, calmness, and serenity of 'their lake' erase Tom's stress.

The first Martini slowed down the negative thoughts racing in Tom's mind, and the second removed them. He was able to enjoy a relaxed dinner with the wife and children that were so dear to him.

Relaxed and at peace, Liz, lead Tom upstairs at 9:30 p.m. and they slowly and tenderly enjoyed passion.

Gratuitously, no calls disrupted Tom's sleep and he awoke at 6 a.m., feeling rested and eager to go back into battle. He bounded out of bed and went downstairs, still dressed in his red and black checkered pajamas. The coffee maker had been set the previous evening, for six, so freshly brewed coffee was waiting. He poured a mug full, then, went out on the deck to savor the morning sunrise. The sun was slowly pushing its way over the Green Mountains of Vermont. Sol's rays commenced stretching across the surface of the lake, causing a phenomenon that was beautiful and inspiring. It appeared that millions of diamonds were lying on the surface of the lake and they glittered, gleamed and sparkled brilliantly. The magnificent living artistry caused Tom to utter, "Thank you Dear God! Your ironic artistry is greatly appreciated and no human artist could create such a majestic vista." He opted to stand on the deck rather than sit, slowly savoring his coffee while marveling at the beauty of 'his lake.' After the sun had risen above the mountains, the display of gems on the lake dissipated and he switched his focus to the 36 nest, white bird house sitting atop a pole at lawn's edge. The avian inn was vacant at this time of year and gave the appearance of a lone sentinel at water's edge. From mid April to August of every year, the white bird inn, or condo, having a green roof, became a hub of avian activity, as Purple Martin wayfarers arrived from South America, to enjoy their summer vacation in North America. The Martins were a joy to watch as they were very social and their diet consisted solely of insects. Early morning and late afternoon was their favorite meal time. Martins exited their summer abodes, stretched their wings on the small terrace fronting their entrance and then swooped out over the lake searching for breakfast, or dinner. Of course, there was always an abundance of food. As they took off they chirped a greeting to the world and then soared and swooped over the lake, gathering insects in their beaks, often slapping the lake surface to snare a tidbit trying to escape them. Soon after arriving for their summer vacation, the all black female Martins laid their eggs and stayed atop the eggs throughout most of the day. During this time of nesting and hatching, the handsome, purple breasted male Martins were required to bring in the 'bacon', or in this case 'the bugs.'

Post dinner every evening, the birds socialized on the terraces fronting their abodes. They conversed in the 'chirp' language of Martins and it was a humorous sight to behold. As it was now late September, the Martin house stood silent and appeared lonely. The beautiful, little avian, 'Snow birds' – as Tom referred to them – because like so many folks living in the north who went south every winter, the Martins returned to wherever they wintered in South America. It saddened Tom to see the empty Martin house; however, he knew that with the arrival of spring his feathery friends would return. While reflecting on the Martins, the haunting cry of loons assailed his ears, and sent a shiver up his spine. The loons talking to each other were out of sight; however, he tracked the sound to the Cliff Haven cove, just four houses away. While savoring the beauty and serenity of the lake, he could put all thoughts of police work out of mind. Although unrealized, the beauty of Lake Champlain was a form of therapy for him. His reverie was suddenly interrupted by someone calling to him.

"Good morning Tom, you are up and about early." The greeting came from Jack Purl, his next door neighbor, also out on his deck. Jack was a retired Air Force Colonel, and he and wife Margaret (Maggie), were long time residents of Cliff Haven, having purchased their home while Jack was still in the Air Force, and transferred to Plattsburgh AF Base. Like Tom and Liz Weston, the Purl's were Roman Catholic and had a slew of kids. Colonel Jack was a proud alumnus of Notre Dame University and it made him proud to profess to everyone he came in contact with, that all eight of his children had also graduated from Notre Dame. At 74 years of age, Jack maintained a slim physique, beneath a youthful appearing face, head topped by a salt and pepper crew cut. In retirement he was an avid golfer and most week days he could be found at Bluff Point Golf Course, located just a half-mile south of Cliff Haven. During late Spring-Summer and Fall Jack spent most weekends fishing from his 16-foot Bay-Liner, on Lake Champlain. Grey-haired and somewhat overweight, Maggie Purl, possessed a happy-carefree personality and was attractive in many ways. Jack and Maggie Purl were very much in love and devoted to each other despite the fact that Maggie was a home-body and did not participate in her husband's activities. She detested exercise, but loved entertaining family and friends. Otherwise, she was perfectly content to maintain her home and spent her spare time knitting garments for grandchildren. While polar opposites in physical appearance, Maggie Purl and Liz Weston, had two things in common. Neither gave a hoot for the game of golf, and both considered fishing a waste of time. Maggie was devoted to her husband of 48-years and though detesting smoking and worrying about his daily consumption of vodka, she tolerated both habits and did not nag him about either.

"Hey Jack," Tom replied. "Good morning back at you. You caught me out here in my P.J.'s."

"At least you are covered up," Jack called back, then, added, "Being as you were out on the lake late last night I am surprised to see you at this early hour."

Puzzled by Jack's statement, Tom responded, "You must be mistaken, Jack, I didn't go out on the lake last night."

"Guess I was seeing things," Jack replied. "I couldn't get to sleep last night, so stepped out on my deck to grab a smoke – you know Maggie doesn't like me smoking in the house. Anyway, while I was out there, I could swear I saw you, or someone, on your boat, at your mooring. Looked to me that you had just tied up at your mooring and was using a flashlight to snap on your boat canvas. If you weren't out there, maybe I should consider switching to a different brand of Vodka." He changed the subject, "We've been watching the news and it is terribly depressing; thousands of good folks killed by those Moslem terrorists, and a lot of killing going on right here in Clinton County. You must be very busy Tom?"

"Too darned busy, Jack, the finding of those gold coins in the lake, as well as the discovery that 'Champ' is real and alive, touched off a spate of death and destruction. We thought we had the man responsible salted away, but he escaped from jail. Nothing that you and Maggie have to worry about though, and I am optimistic we will soon re-capture him. I am curious, what time did you observe the activity on my boat?"

"About one-thirty, as I said was having difficulty getting to sleep. Come to think about it, you must be working a lot of hours and don't have much time to go out on the lake. Perhaps it was Rabideau, his mooring is next to yours. But, I don't think so, because his boat is bigger than yours."

"Could be, and yes Jack, I am working a lot of hours and

grateful for the brief respite this morning. The beauty of 'our' lake is a real stress reliever. It has been nice chatting with you, but I have to leave this serenity and get back to work. I hope you score well today and beat your golfing partners."

"Thanks Tom! Good luck catching that killer creep, and say hello to Liz for us."

"Will do Jack, and same to Maggie." Tom re-entered his home, kissed Liz, who was preparing breakfast in the kitchen, then went upstairs to clean up and dress for work. While getting dressed, he reflected on Jack's initial conversation about seeing 'someone' with a flashlight on his boat. *He was probably mistaken, and his intake of Vodka caused his imagination to kick in. Yet, why is it troubling me. I think I will go check on 'Hav-n-Fun' before I head off to work.* He removed the tan slacks he intended to wear to the office, and donned a pair of shorts, topped by a tee shirt. When he returned downstairs to eat breakfast, Liz gave him a puzzled look and stated, "My-oh-my, are you working undercover today?"

"No honey," Tom replied, "I spoke with our neighbor while out on the deck this morning and he told me he 'thought' he saw 'someone' on our boat at about 1:30 this morning. I am sure he is mistaken, but my cop curiosity causes me to want to go check our boat, before I go to the station."

After concluding breakfast, Tom left the house, went down the stairs leading to the lakeshore, turned over his canoe and paddled out to *Hav-n-Fun's* mooring. He first examined the boat's exterior and saw nothing wrong. The canvas panels enclosing the cabin were intact and zippered properly. Then, he unzipped the canvas covering the aft section and clambered on board. He scanned the boat's cabin and everything appeared intact. Then he unlatched the hooks that secured the hatch cover covering the 264 horse power inboard motor. What he saw caused his hands to start shaking and he felt a sudden chill. He immediately recognized the four tubular objects bound together with duct tape, lying atop the engine, as sticks of dynamite. A blasting cap was attached and wired to the boat's ignition switch. If he had decided to start the motor before examining it, he would have become another victim in Bashoul's reign of terror. While staring at the bomb, he uttered a sigh and thought, *Dear God, thank you! You sent Jack out on his deck last night to smoke that cigarette, because you are protecting me and my family. Then you inspired both Jack and I to go out on our decks this morning to engage in conversation. I owe you big time! If that twist of irony had not occurred, I, and possibly Liz and our children, would have become fish bait.* He said aloud, "Damn you Bashoul! Now, I definitely want you dead!" The uncertainty of another back-up explosive device caused Tom to replace the hood covering the boat's engine. He then returned to shore and before entering his home, knocked on his neighbor's door. He was in luck as Jack had not yet departed for the golf course.

"Hey Tom, what's up," he greeted?

"Jack, that smoke, you took on your deck last night, resulting in your observation of someone on my boat, then, reporting what you saw to me this morning, saved my life and possibly the lives of my family. I owe you a debt of gratitude and you will forever be in my prayers."

Jack looked puzzled. "What is this all about, Tom? What did you find?"

"Someone planted a bomb, wired to my boat's ignition. If I had inserted the key and turned the engine over, *Hav-n-Fun* and whoever was on board would have been blasted to bits. Thank you, Jack, for reporting what you saw last night to me this morning. Please don't go near my boat until I give you the okay. Please reflect again on what you observed last night. When you saw the activity on my boat, did you notice anything else?"

Jack rubbed his chin as he sought recall of the previous

night. Finally, he answered, "Maggie and I went to bed after watching the eleven o'clock news. She went right off to sleep, but I felt irritable and bothered by something, and was having difficulty figuring out what was bothering me. I got up, worked on a crossword puzzle, thinking that would tire me out. It didn't. Eventually, probably around one-one-thirty, I decided that having a smoke would settle me down. I went out on the deck and as I was lighting up, I heard a cough – or, was it a sneeze – out on the lake, quite near shore. I walked to the edge of my deck to see if I could make out where the sound came from. It was then I noticed a person – I thought it was you – on your boat. The individual had a small flashlight and appeared to be zippering your aft canvas. There was a small dingy at the back of your boat and I just assumed you had been out on the lake and just came in. I didn't yell hello, because didn't want to awaken anyone."

"Well, Jack, count your blessings that you didn't. If you had, you very well could have become another homicide victim. I've got to believe our Good Lord is watching over me – and perhaps you. Perhaps 'He' was the cause of your sleeplessness and inspiration to go out for a smoke. Whatever, the reason, you my dear neighbor, my dear man, saved my life! I owe you big time."

Jack displayed a huge smile as he answered, "Just pleased and happy my favorite neighbor and favorite cop is okay – also, that his family is okay."

As Tom re-entered the house, Liz flashed her husband a smile and immediately asked, "Is everything okay on the boat?"

"Not really, Honey! But, I don't want to alarm or frighten you."

Liz's smile immediately disappeared to be replaced by a concerned frown. "What is it Tom? What did you find?"

Before answering, Tom approached his wife, took her in his arms and then calmly answered, "Someone placed a bomb on our dear *Hav-n-Fun*. Four sticks of dynamite were on the motor and wired so as to explode when I turned the ignition key. Thank God, Jack went out on his deck last night to grab a smoke, thought he saw me on our boat and told me about his observations this morning. Otherwise, I, or possibly all of us, would have been killed. It is obvious who ordered the bomb placed on our boat and from now on love, we have to be extra cautious. Bashoul, is apparently hell-bent on killing me, and taking out you and our children would be a bonus. I don't want you or our kids leaving home without a security escort."

Tears commenced flowing down Liz's cheeks and she responded in a choked up whisper, "Oh no! Oh God no! Tom, please retire! We must escape this nightmare! I could not bear to lose you, or any of our children! My life would become an empty void and I would become an emotional and physical wreck. Please, retire! Let someone else go after that madman!"

Tom wrapped his arms around his wife and gently stroked her hair as he tried to bolster her strength and reassure her that everything would be okay. He spoke quietly to her in a reassuring whisper, "Honey, we will be okay. Nothing is going to happen to you, Mary, Susan, Jeremy, Bobby, or Joe, and having failed in this attempt, I do not believe Bashoul will try again. Stay strong my love! It is only a matter of time until we get Bashoul and then the nightmare – like all ugly dreams – will come to an end. Now, I'm going to call the supervisor of our bomb squad and *Hav-n-Fun* will become safe again."

Tom called Sergeant James Fleming, supervisor of Troop B's 'Explosive and Demolition Team' from home. He explained his dilemma and was assured the bomb would be disarmed A.S.A.P.

Tom's next call was to Red Whalen at the Plattsburgh state police station. Tom explained to Red why he was late coming in, asked Red to contact Zone and Troop officers and advise them what had happened. When this was taken care of, he called his nephew and told him not to go anywhere, or do anything until "Investigators Hermione and Rasmussen are stuck to you like glue."

Tom waited at home for Sergeant Fleming, who arrived at 9:40 a.m. Fleming had entered the New York State Police after serving a hitch in Army Special Forces. He managed to get into the state police just under the maximum age wire and now had ten years service. Having a military background as an 'explosives and demolition expert' turned him into a valuable asset for the state police. Though he was only 41-years old, premature grey hair and a slight limp caused Fleming to appear 50-. The limp came about as a result of Fleming's negotiations with a nut case, who was wearing a vest loaded with explosive and intent on killing himself and co-workers. On scene troopers had called Fleming, who responded and tried to talk the despondent, suicidal, car salesman into giving up the remote that would trigger the device. He failed in that regard and having misjudged the potency of the explosive charge and its danger zone caught some shrapnel when the nut job triggered the device. Fortunately, Fleming had managed to capture the attention of the perpetrator and his intended targets managed to escape while their assailant was talking with Fleming.

Tom explained what he observed on *Hav-n-Fun,* and then took the Sergeant out to his boat in his canoe. Fleming directed Tom to return to shore and wait safely there while he defused the bomb. After the bomb was disconnected, he would signal Tom to come back and get him. Fortunately upon observing the dynamite bomb, Fleming knew exactly how to disarm it, and Tom had no more than returned to shore, when Fleming signaled to come back out and get him.

Fleming placed the sticks of dynamite in a specially designed container, resembling a beer cooler, and placed the container in his truck. He explained that he disarmed the bomb by disconnecting the wire connected to the boat's ignition switch. He also advised that he had taken photographs of the device, before and after disarmament. Also, that he had examined the interior of the boat cabin and did not find any other potentially dangerous device or dangerous substance.

Tom invited Fleming into his home for coffee, but the Sergeant declined, advising he had to go to Ray Brook, dispose of the dynamite, and then report to the firing range for annual firearms qualification. He would take Tom up on his offer another time.

Liz was relieved to learn the bomb was gone and her husband and their boat were now safe – at least for the time being; however, worry and concern were taking a toll on her. The former Peru High School cheerleader and 'Miss Clinton County' beauty queen; married 25 years and mother of five children, at age 46 years, retained her youthful beauty and maintained a trim figure. Not a member of any health clubs, and not an exercise fanatic, Liz attributed her looks, health and physical condition to love, happiness, security and having a strong faith in God. For the first time in her life, she was worried – not about herself, but the safety and security of the man she deeply loved and the safety of their children. Prior to Stan LaPierre being murdered and Jack nearly murdered, she was a happy, always smiling woman, considering herself blessed among women. She and Tom had dated while they were in high school and the tall, handsome athlete, with adorable blue eyes and warm, sincere smile, captured her heart. When Tom joined the Marine Corps, they corresponded on a weekly basis and she prayed on a daily basis that he would return to her healthy and in possession of the same adorable personality. Her prayers were granted and soon after Tom's discharge from the Corps, they took their marriage vows at St. Augustine Church, in their hometown of Peru. She had supported Tom's decision to join the

New York State Police, and as she watched her handsome husband in his grey uniform, walk across the stage of Albany's Palace Theater to accept his diploma, she was filled with pride. She realized that there were risks and dangers in the police profession, but she trusted in her husband's ability to avoid injury and not take unneeded risk. During the 25-years her husband had served as uniform Trooper, Investigator and now Senior Investigator, he had arrived home from work uninjured and she gave thanks to God on a daily basis for protecting him. She also knew that Tom had obviously been involved in dangerous situations, but he did not share details of those incidences with her and she was content in not knowing about them.

Of course none of the crimes her husband investigated, nor, criminals he was seeking to arrest had personally affected nor impacted the safety of the Weston family until this Muslim madman Bashoul surfaced. For the first time during her husband's long career, worry and concern were eating at Liz's conscience and causing her stress. She was not eating properly. She was sleep deprived and worry lines now appeared on her formerly youthful, happy face. She was starting to lose weight and worked at trying to conceal that fact from the man she dearly loved. Much of her time was now spent in prayer.

While waiting for Sergeant Fleming to arrive, Troopers Mitchell Long and Patricia Harmon arrived at the Weston home and advised they had been assigned to provide security for Liz and the Weston's children during the day. They requested that the family remain confined to home, for the duration of the investigation to apprehend Bashoul. Tom requested that Liz and their kids heed all direction from the security team. He was going to arrange for their children's school work to be assigned via internet and email.

Tom knew both Long and Harmon and as the two young

troopers were somewhat in awe and respected him, was sure that they would do their best to protect his family from harm.

Twenty-two year old Patty Harmon had been in the state police one year and was in excellent physical condition. Patty kept her long dark hair tied in a bun, beneath the Stetson that completed the full state police uniform. Harmon had become close friends with Patty Hermione, after being assigned to Plattsburgh and the two Patty's practiced martial arts together. Though appearing slim, Harmon was muscular and not to be trifled with. Many men who had 'hit' on the young trooper and became overly amorous had to nurse pain as a result of Patty's response.

Though slightly overweight, Trooper Long, standing six-foot-four inches, was an imposing figure, especially when in uniform, with height emphasized by Stetson. The 25- year old Trooper, having wavy brown hair had been in the state police for 4 years, was single, and had no romantic interest; although he was attracted to Trooper Harmon. To this time, he had not expressed his interest to Patty and they had not dated.

Liz was not pleased over this security arrangement, but told Tom she would make the Troopers comfortable and treat them politely.

Tom kissed his scowling wife goodbye, assuring her that Long and Harmon would not get in her way and would be focused on activity in the vicinity of their residence. He smiled and told her, "Honey, I hope to be home by 7."

The Plattsburgh station was still being used as command post and everyone gathered there was eager to learn about the bomb planted on Tom's boat. How did he learn it was on the boat? What type of bomb was it? How was it set? What was his wife's reaction when learning about the bomb? They asked questions about Sergeant Fleming, and welcomed Tom with embraces. After learning how Tom found out that someone had been on his boat, they mutually agreed that the Good Lord must be watching out for him. How fortunate his neighbor had gone out on his deck for a mid night smoke and saw the activity. Fortunate again that Tom went out on his deck before heading off to work and was hailed by his neighbor. Members of his squad expressed concern that when Bashoul learned the attempt to kill Tom, via the placement of a bomb on his boat had failed, he would try again, as he obviously held a deep hatred for their boss. Tom shrugged off their concern and suggested they needed to be concerned about their own safety and constantly be on guard. It was decided that the attempt on Tom's life would not be reported to the media. They wanted Bashoul to believe that Tom would be killed when he started his boat.

Major O'Neill summed up the feelings shared by many in the room: "Tom, you are one mighty lucky trooper. The 'Man' up in Heaven must not want you up there yet. Remind me not to play poker with you, because you've got 'The Almighty' watching out for you."

The Major's statement elicited a chuckle from Tom, who responded, "I give thanks and hope my luck holds for a few more years. I've got to hang around to prevent any of you Casanova's from going after my beautiful widow and, I've got to get five kids through college.

I don't know why Our Lord is watching out for a sinner like me and guess it is high time for me to go to Confession. What really troubles me, is how did Bashoul know *Hav-n-Fun* was my boat? There are 20 or more boats moored in our cove. I know he is extremely intelligent, but is he psychic too?" He looked around the room for an answer.

"I think I know the answer, Boss," Red Whalen replied. "Do you remember, following the fraudulent obituary concerning Jack's death, published in the Plattsburgh Press-Republican?" He continued, without waiting for an answer. "I've got the article in my desk drawer, wait just a minute while I get it." Five minutes later he was reading from the article: "It was reported that New York State Police Senior Investigator Tom Weston, supervisor of the Plattsburgh BCI unit, now has more than 20-years in the state police. Weston resides with his wife and five children in Cliff Haven." - skipping over some of the article he continued – "Weston told the Plattsburgh Press-Republican that he enjoys police work and has no immediate plans to retire. When not engaged in solving crime, he enjoys cruising beautiful Lake Champlain on his boat *Hav-n-Fun.*"

"Well, I'll be damned," Tom responded! "I had forgotten about that article. Apparently, Bashoul keeps up with Plattsburgh news by not only watching Channel 5, but by reading the Plattsburgh Press-Republican. Hmm, I wonder if he would be foolish enough to have a subscription. Red, please give a call to the paper's circulation desk and ask if they have a customer by the name of Omar Bashoul, or Abdul Markesh?"

"Will do Boss, but I wouldn't get my hopes up."

"I know Red, but we have to touch every base in our hunt for the scumbag. You might also ask them to provide the names of any subscribed customers in Montreal and Quebec. You know many Canadians are interested in Plattsburgh news and in conversation with Scott McCormick, he told me that this past summer, after Omar became a suspect in LaPierre's murder, he took out a subscription. There is a slim possibility that one of Bashoul's cronies is getting the paper for his revered Imam."

"You got it Boss, and any subscribers having a Muslim name will be of special interest."

12

The hours became days and the days passed with no information or evidence developed that would aid in capturing Omar Bashoul. Frustration was mounting and the bill for police overtime was beginning to gnaw at Major O'Neill, who had begun receiving tepid heat from headquarters in Albany. Superintendent Grayson, requested a daily report from Major O'Neill as to the progress of the investigation, and suggested that he cut back on the number of personnel involved in the investigation until such time more substantive information was developed.

Frustration was also mounting in a cabin located in the woods in New Hampshire. Omar Bashoul, was a man of action, and not accustomed to rural solitude. He also knew that he could not communicate via phone, as he knew phone communications – especially cell phone – were easily traceable. He communicated with trusted followers via his secret assistant, Muhammed Moosha. Moosha had followed Bashoul to Canada, as a back up to Bashoul. In the event Bashoul became unable to assist the young jihadists in America, Moosha would take over. Though friends and both devoted followers of Osama Bin Laden, they pretended to hardly know each other. A native of Saudi Arabia, 36-year old Moosha was a medical doctor, and general practitioner. He was admitted to Canada in 1998, and established his medical practice in Montreal. Most of his patients were Muslims and most were affiliated with the Khalil Mosque, where Omar Bashoul was Imam. Virtually no one was aware that Imam Bashoul and Doctor Moosha, were partners in plotting to kill Americans, and why would they as the pudgy, soft spoken Doctor, exhibiting a habitual smile and having a friendly demeanor, seemed the antithesis of the tall, ruggedly built, often critical Imam.

While collaborating with Moosha, Abdul asked that Moosha purchase the Plattsburgh Press-Republican newspaper on a daily basis and have the paper delivered to him at the cabin. He stated, "I have cable service in the cabin and am able to watch the news; however, the visual media does not include tidbits of personal information concerning Weston and other infidels in that area that I need to know about. I am eagerly looking forward to reading Weston's obituary."

"I have subscribed to the newspaper Imam," Moosha eventually responded, "and I will have it delivered into your hands. What other requests do you have for your humble servant?"

"Moosha, the authorities will focus their efforts and dig deep to turn up information connecting members of my Mosque to me. I trust that if questioned, 'our' loyal soldiers will not tell the infidels anything. They will only admit to attending the Khalil Mosque where I am Imam. Of course, you are now my contact with our soldiers, should we be concerned they will focus on our relationship?"

"Great Imam, I believe the authorities will only connect my association with any of 'our' soldiers as doctor-patient. I do not call on patients, they come to my office and that is where I give them their assignments. Also, if the authorities do call on me, you are probably aware that legally, doctor-patient relationships are held to be confidential by the courts. I will tell the infidels nothing."

"My Dear Moosha, you are not only brilliant, but clever as well. You must be prepared because I have been mulling over the need to create more mayhem that will overwhelm American law enforcement. We need to keep them so busy they cannot focus full attention on finding an elusive Imam."

Moosha smiled in response then asked, "When do you plan to leave and rejoin Osama?"

"When my work is finished here, and when the time is right. How many fine jihadists can we count on to continue the holy war?"

"Several Imam, I intend to use one of our most loyal and trusted brothers, Ahmed Gasmani to bring you the newspaper and relay your instructions to me."

"Ahmed is an excellent choice, Dear Moosha. I am pleased."

It was out of character for an active Imam to while away time in an isolated cabin. Omar missed the Khalid Mosque; he missed leading daily prayer; he missed the adulation he received from Montreal's Muslim community; he missed his precious Koran, and most of all he missed Jazine 'The Flower of Mecca,' his devoted mistress. She was dutifully operating Abdul's Specialty Store in his absence. He trusted that the authorities would have no cause to arrest Jazine and if questioned, she would tell them she had no idea where Bashoul was – and, she didn't. Omar dealt with boredom by praying five times each day to Allah, and asked Allah to give him guidance in devising plots to destroy non-believers. Devising plots to do away with those responsible for disrupting his former idyllic life took precedence. To monitor the police investigation to capture him, he tuned in to local television news reports, and read newspapers.

Bashoul was quite pleased and proud with his genius which after recalling an article published in the Plattsburgh Press-Republican, inspired the means of eliminating Tom Weston. His plot to kill Angus Horban, via explosives had worked out very well, so why not take out Tom Weston, in the same manner. As Kahil had performed magnificently in executing the plan to take out Horban, he decided to use Kahil again to plant the bomb that would destroy Weston. As a loyal follower and potential jihadist, Kahil would ask for no payment; however, in considering that he would want to call on Kahil again, Bashoul offered him $10,000, a small price to pay to get rid of that arrogant police officer.

Two days had passed by since Kahil reported that the bomb had been placed on Weston's boat, and no reporting of Weston's death. Bashoul knew that the report of a bomb exploding on a boat in Cliff Haven, taking the life of a well-known police officer, would be big News and he was eagerly watching for that report. He thought, *Apparently, Weston is so busy looking for me he hasn't had the time or opportunity to go boating.* He smiled while envisioning the surprise awaiting the arrogant, self-assured American police officer. It was time to also surprise the nephew.

13

The hours became days and the days passed in frustration as no information or evidence came in to aid in locating and capturing Bashoul.

Troopers were assigned as security for Liz Weston and the Weston children. Patty Hermione and Troy Rasmussen were shadowing Jack Weston. Jack was completing his final week as manager of the Subway store. He was eagerly looking forward to becoming a member of the Clinton County Sheriff's Department, embarking on a career in law enforcement and marrying Kathleen Kelly, the woman he had sworn his love to five years ago. Anxious to close out his last day of employment at Subway, he kept glancing at the clock above the store's entrance waiting for that moment when he could shout 'hooray!'

The clock was approaching 10 p.m. and Jack Weston began the process of auditing the day's receipts, so he could lock up the premises for the last time. Suddenly, two swarthy in appearance young men dressed in black chinos and black vinyl jackets entered the store and approached the counter. They glanced briefly at the two customers seated at tables in the dining area, then turned their attention on the attendant behind the register. They focused on this individual as he matched the description of the man they were looking for, and appeared to be the only employee in the store. The female customer seated at a table on one side of the store and the male customer seated at a table on the opposite side of the store would become consequential victims after they completed their assigned task.

Jack eyed the two men warily as he asked, "Gentlemen, how may I help you?"

The apparent leader of the pair smiled in return and asked, "Are you Jack Weston?"

"As a matter-of-fact, I am," Jack replied.

Having heard the desired answer, both men reached behind the jackets that concealed holstered handguns and drew their weapons. While raising them, the leader shouted out, "Prepare to die Infidel Wes-"

Before he finished pronouncing Weston, two shots rang out simultaneously. A look of shock and surprise was the last semblance of life on the two assassin's faces as they crumpled to the floor. Neither of the assassins had anticipated difficulty in carrying out their mission and both were stunned and surprised by the explosion of guns that were not theirs, followed by searing pain that expedited their travel to the imagined Muslim paradise; whether it be Heaven or Hell. Both shots had been well placed and blood commenced pooling on the floor around both men.

Upon seeing the two men draw weapons from a holster on their waist, Patty and Troy sprang into action cutting down the two with well aimed shots from 40-calibre Smith and Wesson's. Everything happened so quickly, Jack was stunned and shaken.

Having saved Jack's life, Patty Hermione and Troy Rasmussen, knelt to examine both victim's. Satisfied that they were dead, Patty calmly asked, "Are you okay Jack?"

Mouth agape, Jack responded in a choked whisper, "I'm okay! If not for your quick action, I would be dead! Oh my God! When is this nightmare going to end?" He collapsed in a chair, placed his hands over his face and sat shaking in silence.

Troy, who had remained silent throughout the incident, now gazed into Patty's eyes, giving her a look of worry and concern. His body was shaking as he asked, "What about you Patty? Are you okay?"

Patty holstered her weapon, placed both arms around Troy's neck, and whispered, "I am okay Troy. These animals were intent on killing Jack, and we did what we had to do. Think back to that day at the hospital. We did what we had to do that day as well, and we suffered guilt feelings for days afterwards. We must not let this eat at our conscience. Our job is to protect Jack and in doing so, we were forced to shoot animals intent on killing him. Don't let it eat at you! I will call 'it' in."

Patty called the Plattsburgh station on her cell phone. She reported the assassination attempt to Dispatcher Gail Munson, who was working the desk. "Gail, Troy and I are at the Plattsburgh Subway Store. Two men came in intent on killing Jack. It was necessary for Troy and I to shoot them. Please call all the required 'people' and ask Senior Investigator Weston and Doc Hartigan to respond to the Subway Store." She added, "As I am speaking with you, the City Police have arrived. We will advise them what happened and ask for their assistance in protecting the scene. Please call Weston first and ask him to get here A.S.A.P."

Tom had just crawled into bed, when the instrument of torture on the stand beside his bed sounded. Upon answering he was greeted by Plattsburgh Dispatcher Gail Munson. The tone of her voice immediately indicated she was not conveying good news. "Sorry to bother you Senior," was her opening, "Investigator Hermione just called me and asked that you be advised that there has been an attempt on your nephew's life. I know few details and she asked that you go to the Subway store and meet Coroner Hartigan there."

"Oh no," Tom groaned! "What about Jack? Is he okay? Where are Patty and Troy? Are they okay?"

"Senior, as previously indicated, I was not provided much detail. Perhaps you might want to call Investigator Hermione on her cell. Do you have her number?"

"Yes, Gail. Rather than calling, I will go right to the store. Please make sure Doc Hartigan is contacted and then call all the required brass. After I get there, I will evaluate what is needed and give you a shout."

Having heard the phone, Liz was sitting up in bed and stated, "By the sound of your conversation, that was not good news and my husband is about to abandon me again."

Having hung up the phone, Tom turned to his wife, nodded his head in the affirmative and trying to soften the message responded, "Honey, 'they' have tried to kill Jack again, fortunately, Patty and Troy prevented that from happening. Apparently it was necessary to shoot Jack's attackers. They need me there and I will give you a call to let you know Jack's condition after I learn all the details. I'm sorry love! I know your night's sleep is now ruined, but try to rest and not worry."

Tears started flowing from Liz's eyes and her body started shaking. Lifting her legs, she wrapped her arms around her knees and rocked back and forth while moaning, "Tom, this nightmare has got to come to an end. This evil being - the one you refer to as Bashoul – is determined to kill you and Jack. Please, Oh God, please Tom, let us escape this nightmare! Retire and let someone else worry about capturing him; please, for my sake, and the sake of our children, retire and let's get away from here."

Tom wrapped his arms around his now sobbing wife and whispered, "Liz – Elizabeth Ewald Weston – you are dear and precious to me and it does tear me apart to see you so distraught. Believe me, I want out of this nightmare as much as you, but we cannot just run away from it. It will just haunt us wherever we go. The only way to deal with this evil monster is to send him back to Hell, where he apparently crawled out of. Liz, honey, I need you to stay strong. I believe the Good Lord is watching over us and will continue to shield us. My Love, we will put an end to the nightmare! Stay focused on our love and keeping our children happy and stress free. I will give you a call before I leave the Subway. On my way to the Subway store, I will call Helen and ask her to come and spend the day with you. She will be concerned about Jack, and you can give strength to each other." Giving his wife a kiss on her forehead, he got out of bed and rushed to get dressed.

During the short drive to Subway, Tom wondered how Patty and Troy were holding up. This was their 2nd fatal shooting while protecting Jack. After the conclusion of their first shooting - at Champlain Valley Physician's Hospital (CVPH), both claimed to be emotionally okay; however, in required follow up counseling, it became obvious that having killed someone was gnawing at their conscience. Although both shootings were totally justified and necessary to preserve life, having killed another human being weighed on their mind. Tom focused on offering both constant reassurances that neither man, nor God, condemned them for doing their duty.

Tom arrived at the Subway Store before Coroner Hartigan. The Plattsburgh police had placed yellow crime scene tape around the store and two uniform officers were preventing entry to the store by members of the media and the public. Tom found a parking place in the shopping plaza parking lot about 200 yards from the Subway and walked to the store. As he approached, he shook his head in disgust. Channel 5's 'Sexy, drop-dead gorgeous' Susan James accompanied by a camera crew had beaten him to the crime scene.

Susan spotted Tom approaching and shoved a microphone in his face. "Investigator Weston, can you tell the people of the North Country about the shooting that took place here this evening?"

Shielding anger and disgust, Tom responded carefully, "Ma'am," (he knew that James would not like being referred to as ma'am), "As you can see, I am just arriving and do not have any details to report at this time. The Coroner and State Police forensic specialists have been called and after we conclude our investigation here, 'we' will provide an in-depth release. Now please excuse me, I have work to do." He pushed the microphone away, and ducked under the crime scene tape.

The Subway store was small, consisting of perhaps three hundred square feet. Tom glanced about the interior and saw Jack, Patty and Troy, seated at a table in one corner of the dining area. The bodies of two individuals were lying in a pool of blood, on the tile floor in the proximity of the service counter. He walked to the table where his nephew and the investigators were seated and as he approached they stood up. He embraced each one before uttering a word. His first words were: "Are you all okay?"

All three nodded their heads in the affirmative. Patty spoke, "We had no choice Boss! They came in, approached Jack and asked if he was Jack Weston. When he acknowledged that he was, they both drew weapons. Troy and I recognized that yelling at them to drop their guns would have had no effect on them. We had to shoot before they did." She paused for a moment and then added, "They are both young and appear to be middle-eastern."

"Damned Bashoul has his hooks into a lot of followers," Tom growled in reply. "The important result of this is that Jack is okay, you and Troy are okay; you performed well and were entirely justified in doing what you had to do. I am sure that when our identification folks get here they will find nothing to the contrary. They will bag the deceased's hands and fingerprint them in the morgue. It is my guess both of these thugs came down from Canada and I am hopeful Scott McCormick and his folks will be able to tell us their identity. Also hopeful identifying them will help connect the dots leading to Bashoul." Directing his attention to Patty and Troy, he continued, "As you are aware, because your weapons were used, they have to be temporarily turned over for examination. I am not going to ask for them here because – as evil as that SOB Bashoul is – you may have-need, to use them again on your way to the station. You can hold onto them for now and turn them over to Captain Burrows at the station. I will hold things down here until our identification folks arrive. Please take Jack down to our station and stick to him like glue. When you get in the office, report to Red Whalen and I will have him take your depositions. I will see you later, any concerns or questions?"

All three shook their heads in the negative. As they stood hugs were again exchanged. As Jack, Patty and Troy started for the door, Tom added, "Oh, by the way, you will probably be confronted by Susan James and her camera crew when you go outside. Just say you have no comment and push them aside."

When Coroner Hartigan arrived at the scene, he examined both victims and ordered their removal to the Plattsburgh morgue, after the Troop B forensics team completed processing the crime scene. "Damn it Weston," he complained! "How many times have I got to tell you, I'm getting tired of getting called out in the middle of the night! When in hell are you going to arrest that Abdul character?"

Tom shook his head in the negative as he responded, "Doc, I am just as tired and frustrated as you. I am also very pissed that a pile of living excrement is trying very hard to kill Jack, me, and many other innocent folks. Believe me, we are pulling out all stops to locate and apply cuffs to that asshole. Perhaps identification of these two thugs will put us on the right path. We will just have to keep plugging along and grin and bear it for now."

Troop B Identification Bureau Forensic Specialist Claire Martin, arrived at the Plattsburgh morgue shortly after both of the victims arrived there. Coroner Hartigan and Tom were in the morgue when she arrived. Both greeted her with smiles and Doc said, "We've got to stop meeting like this. Investigator, there is a hell-of-a lot of killing going on and frankly, I'm getting sick of it."

Claire smiled in return as she responded, "You are right Doc. I was under the impression my work in forensics would be mostly a day job. Since this Bashoul started making his evil presence known in the North Country, we have been very busy, both day and night."

Claire photographed both victims and then took their fingerprints.

"No question as to what killed them," Hartigan stated as Claire took prints. "Two well placed heart shots. Our challenge now is to identify these thug's and I hope those prints you are taking will do the trick." Changing the subject he added, "They appear to be Muslim and as they were obviously sent by Bashoul, that is a given. They're both young, probably in their 20's. I would lay odds they came down from Montreal. What do you think?"

"I wouldn't bet against it," Tom answered. "Claire, I would appreciate your faxing those prints up to Scott McCormick. I will give you the number. Hopefully, the RCMP will be able to identify them for us." Turning attention to Coroner Hartigan, he added, "When you examined their clothing, did you find anything helpful?"

"Nope, neither was carrying a wallet or identification. Both had a quantity of cash in their pocket."

"Someone must have dropped them off to do their dirty work," Tom added. "No car keys on them either."

The attempt on Jack Weston's life would be reported to the media as an "attempted robbery," resulting in the State Police and Plattsburgh Police being bombarded by questions as to whether they were withholding the true motive for the incident. Chanel #5's Susan James was especially skeptical of the information received and insinuated that the authorities had applied a false label to a deliberate assassination attempt on Jack Weston.

She reported: "Channel 5 questions the accuracy of the report provided by authorities that the fatal shooting of two Montreal men by off-duty state troopers at Plattsburgh's Subway Shop, was the result of a robbery gone bad. Subway Store Manager Jack Weston, soon to become a Clinton County Sheriff's Deputy has been the target of previous attempts on his life, causing question as to whether this evening's shooting – on Mr. Weston's last day of work at the Subway Store, was in fact an attempted robbery, or an attempt on his life? Channel 5 will continue trying to find the answer to that question, as well as answer to the question as to whether the two men shot by Troopers were actually agents of Clinton County Jail escapee Imam Bashoul, whom authorities have been unable to track down."

The front page article in the Plattsburgh Press-Republican reported, "Two armed, off duty, state troopers happened to be eating in the Subway store when two men entered and pulled guns on store manager Jack Weston. Both yet to be identified robbery suspects were shot by the off duty troopers, when they threatened the manager of the store. The manager, Jack Weston, was unarmed and unharmed in the incident. The robbery suspects, - according to sources – both appeared to be middle-eastern men. Although police officials told the Plattsburgh Press Reporter, the incident was an attempted robbery it is of interest that Subway Store Manager Weston was one of the divers who found the treasure trove in Lake Champlain, this past summer. Weston was viciously assaulted in the Peru residence of Stanley LaPierre, by individuals, intent on stealing the treasure found by the divers. LaPierre was murdered during that same incident. The investigation to capture the killers was led by Senior Investigator Tom Weston, of Plattsburgh's State Police, who is the uncle of victim Jack Weston. Investigator Weston falsely reported the death of his nephew to the Plattsburgh Press-Republican, as a ploy to aid in arresting Omar Bashoul, who was subsequently arrested as the individual behind the murder and attempted murder. The criminal charge against Bashoul, alleges that Bashoul's agents tortured both LaPierre and Weston to learn the location of the treasure. During an attempt to recover the golden treasure from a cave located beneath Valcour Island, Bashoul's divers happened upon living and former legend, 'Champ' who killed both divers before they could remove the gold from the cave. The deceased divers were subsequently identified as: Pierre Bouchard, age 38, and Mae Ling Cardin, age 35, both of Montreal, Canada. The Governors of Vermont and New York subsequently granted 'Champ' immunity and issued a declaration proclaiming the 'creature' a protected national treasure.

On September 10, Omar Bashoul was arraigned on the murder charge before Justice Morrisey, in Plattsburgh Town Justice Court, and remanded to the Clinton County jail, pending Grand Jury action. Bashoul escaped from the Clinton County jail, on September 20, during a murderous attack on the facility that resulted in the death of Sheriff's Department members, Sergeant Ted Hughes and Deputy William Hoskins, and Plattsburgh police officers, James Morrow and Jeff Oates. Since his escape, Imam Bashoul has successfully eluded authorities, despite an extensive manhunt. In a twist of irony, the Subway robbery occurred on the last day of store manager Weston's employment. Today, Jack Weston will take the oath of office to become a Clinton County Sheriff's deputy. The New York State Police spokesperson told the Press-Republican that the investigation to apprehend Omar Bashoul is ongoing.

Bashoul placed the newspaper on a table top and commenced pacing about the cabin, while uttering obscenities in Arabic. The Boosha brothers had been devoted followers and he would sorely miss them. *Surely, Allah has welcomed them to paradise. So, Weston suspected another attack on his nephew and assigned security for him. You were lucky this time; however, your luck is going to run out, and next time there will be the added bonus of police infidels.* His mind then shifted to Tom Weston and his thoughts inspired a smile. *Weston, you will soon learn you cannot outwit me.*

Abdul had previously watched the news concerning the Subway shootings, on televisions Channel 5. His hated nemesis New York State Police Senior Investigator Tom Weston was shown being interviewed by Susan James. Weston did not appear very accommodating during the interview and was very brief with his answers. He told James that robbery was the suspected motive for the appearance in the store by the two deceased men. "They choose a very bad time to commit their crime," he said, "because two off duty members of the state police were customers in the store. They were armed and when the robbers drew their weapons, they were shot by the troopers."

You lie with finesse Weston, but soon, you will have the urge to go boating.

Following the attempt on Jack Weston's life, Bashoul sent this message to Moosha, "The authorities will dig deep and turn up much information about the Boosha brothers. Should we be concerned that something exists that connects them to me?"

"Imam," Moosha replied, "that is highly unlikely. I gave them their assignment when they came to my office for an appointment. As we previously discussed, their only connection to you is the

Khalil Mosque and their only connection to me is as doctor/ patient."

As requested, Investigator Martin sent the assassins prints to Sergeant Scott McCormick.

The following day, Scott called Tom. "This is your friendly 'Mountie' from across the border," he greeted. "Please tell me that you know where Omar Bashoul is and his arrest is imminent."

"Hey Scott," Tom responded. "No such luck. That scumbag has covered his tracks well. Do you have some news that will put him in our sights?"

"Not really, but I can tell you who the two punks are that tried to off your nephew. They are – or were – the Boosha brothers, Kahil, age 26, and Mical, age 24. They are – or I should say were – in Canada legally, having emigrated here in 1999. Interestingly, both are enrolled as senior year students at McGill University, Kahil, majoring in physics and Mical, majoring in chemistry. I made some inquiries at the college and was told that neither had attended classes in about two months. We picked up a wealth of information with a visit to the school and conversation with professors and fellow students. Most everyone we spoke with; described the Boosha boys as loners who did not socialize with fellow students, nor, did they participate in school activities. We were told they seemed to be devout in their Islamic faith and regularly attended prayers at the mosque where Bashoul is Imam. Our most interesting interview was with Professor Ernst Brackow, who told us that Kalil was greatly interested in volatile chemicals and explosive material. That caused us to re-examine the Horban assassination and are suspect that Kahil may have been the mysterious limo driver. Using the information you provided me that the Boosha boys; which I might add, were magnificently terminated by your sharpshooting troopers, enabled us to obtain a search warrant for their modest apartment. That was most productive. We found 'how to' build bomb manuals, and writings in Arabic describing planned killings of folks on your side of the border – and wouldn't you know – a limousine driver's uniform. The only thing we found connecting the Boosha's to Bashoul, was a photo of the brother's standing beside him. The photo was autographed by Imam Bashoul, who wrote, "Soldiers of Allah." We now have cause to believe Kahil Boosha, murdered Angus Horban. Please extend my thanks and gratitude to the two officers who excel in the use of firearms. They have saved the Province of Quebec, a lot of money that would have been spent on prosecuting the 'Scamps,' providing them a free defense and the luxury of growing fat in our gaol. I hope this information has been helpful, though we really didn't learn anything that would help in locating Bashoul.

I plan to pay 'Bashoul's mistress' a visit, and will give you a jingle after I do. I also plan on visiting Lisha Ishmani, the young lady that Bashoul sent to Horban, to see if she has any helpful tidbits of information.

What else would you like me to do from this end?"

"You are truly amazing Scott! Your expertise and Sherlock Holmes ability to analyze minute details are immensely helpful. You are already planning the interviews I was going to suggest. I enjoy our chats and look forward to a mutual celebration when Bashoul departs this earth and goes searching for his virgins. Oh, one more thing, after the attempt on me, I wondered how Bashoul knew which boat to plant the bomb on. One of my astute investigators recalled that the name of my boat had appeared in an article in the Plattsburgh Press-Republican. I recall that you told me you subscribed to our newspaper when Bashoul first came into our sights. Investigator Whalen checked with the paper's circulation department and was provided a list of subscribers receiving the paper in Canada. The number of Canucks interested in our news was amazing. The name of a subscriber, living in Montreal, appears to be Muslim. Would you please take a look at him and see if he has any connection to Bashoul?"

"You know, Tom, I would bet that if I checked with the circulation department of the Montreal Gazette, we would learn a lot of folks living down your way are subscribers. Give me this fellow's name and we'll take a peek at him."

"He is a medical doctor Scott, so probably no connection to Bashoul or his group of jihadists, but would appreciate having you check him out. His name is Muhammad Moosha and his newspaper is being delivered at 210 Rue St. Denis. We do not know whether this is his office address or residence."

"I will take a gander at this Doctor and get back to you."

"Thank you Scott! My best wishes to your family."

"Likewise, Tom, Please extend my regards to your lovely wife Liz."

14

One evening while mulling over what sort of destructive diversion he could create to keep the police busy, Omar considered the amenities he appreciated despite being holed up in a log cabin located deep in the New Hampshire woods. He had running water courtesy of a deep well. An electric power line passed through the forest and the cabin had electricity. A cable television service provided access to the visual media and a 40-inch television screen was attached to the wall above the cabin's fireplace. The television was on most of the time as Bashoul wanted to keep up to date on the news. There was also an adequate supply of stacked fire logs to warm the cabin on cool nights.

While planning Bashoul's escape from jail, Moosha found the rental cabin on line, and using a credit card in the name of Gary Brooks, purchased a two month rental. The owner of the cabin lived on Long Island. As an avid hunter, he purchased the New Hampshire cabin for use during the North Country deer season. Intending to have the property basically pay for itself and ensure its upkeep, he decided to rent out the cabin during other times of the year. While in the woods, he had befriended a retired postal worker who was a widower, living about five miles from the cabin. He managed to hire 75-year old Henry Fording to take care of the property. Despite his age, Fording was lean, spry, and took excellent care of his hunting companion's property, including the cutting and stacking of fire wood.

After accepting the rental agreement Fording met Gary Brooks (Moosha), and turned the keys to the cabin over to him. Moosha explained that he was writing a book and wanted the solitude of the woods to focus, concentrate and write. Fording need not visit the cabin during the two month rental, and he would contact Fording to come check the cabin and collect the keys when he was ready to leave. Fording was happy with that arrangement, as he received a monthly check from the owner, for maintaining the cabin.

One evening, while watching television there was an alert that there were severe thunderstorms in the area and residents could expect power outages. The bulletin triggered an idea, as to how Bashoul could create havoc to further engage and confuse the authorities searching for him. He recalled that the Nine Mile Two Nuclear Facility on Lake Ontario, provided electricity to downstate New York, including much of the New York City area. The power was transmitted via lines connected to high metal or steel towers stretching from the nuclear plant upstate, and along the Hudson Valley. During the night he devised a plan which he would have delivered to Moosha via 'their' courier. Now, all he had to do was watch for the results.

A white utility 'bucket' truck parked beside an 80-foot tall, steel electric transmission tower. Two men dressed in white coveralls and wearing orange hard hats exited the vehicle, while the driver remained inside the truck cab. By all appearances, the men were either examining the tower or performing some sort of work. One of the men climbed inside the hydraulic operated bucket and it raised upward approximately thirty-feet. Close observation would reveal he was fastening some sort of object to a tower support; however, there were no close observers. This process was repeated on each leg of the tower support and it would be repeated on the legs of four additional towers. When completed, as the truck moved slowly down the power line, the truck driver pushed a button on a small box located inside the cab of the truck.

The deafening blast from twenty explosive devices exploding at the same time caused some residents in the vicinity of the towers to believe an earthquake was occurring, or bombs were being dropped on America from another group of terrorists. The explosions were deafening and they triggered a shock wave that caused the walls in some homes to crack.

The truck then sped away and proceeded to a highway rest area where the truck was abandoned and its occupants transferred to a car that was waiting for them. As the car exited the rest area, the utility truck exploded scattering debris over a large area.

The collapse of five utility towers brought down the transmission lines and much of downstate New York was suddenly in the dark. Monitors immediately determined that the loss of power was the cause of the collapse of the towers. It was also immediately known that this power outage was no accident but a deliberate act of sabotage.

Fortunately, no one was killed or injured by the work of the saboteurs and fortunately the power was still on in Plattsburgh. It was also fortune or fate that caused dairy farmer Lawrence Heath while repairing his pasture fence on a rise overlooking a highway rest area, to observe a utility truck stop in the rest area. Three men exited the truck and got into a Maroon colored Ford sedan that had its motor running and seemed to be waiting for them. He was curious as to why – what appeared to be utility workers – left their truck, shed reflective vests and helmets, and quickly got into the car. As the car drove out of the parking area Larry removed his cap and scratched his head wondering what the men were up to. In a matter of seconds the answer was provided, as the utility truck exploded and became a flaming pile of debris. Larry reached into the pocket of his jacket, removed a cell phone and dialed 911. His call was answered by an Ulster County Sheriff's Department dispatcher. Larry identified himself, provided his location, reported his bizarre sighting and added, "I don't know what these fellas are up to but it sure in hell is something bad. They left here in a Maroon Ford sedan - about 98 I would guess – and they are headed east on Route 28."

The dispatcher instructed Larry to remain where he was until interviewed in depth by a police officer. The dispatcher followed this instruction with a dispatch to all patrols to be on the lookout for a Maroon Ford sedan, last seen eastbound on Route 28 approximately two miles West of Kingston. It was reported that the vehicle had been observed leaving a Route 28 rest area, immediately following an explosion in the rest area. It was not known whether the occupants of the vehicle were connected to the explosion; however, precaution should be taken. This bulletin was followed by dispatching the Town of Ulster fire department to the rest area. Approximately ten minutes later, Kingston New York Thruway toll booth attendant Mary Hodges, who had heard the radio bulletin, reported to her dispatcher that a 1998 Maroon Ford sedan containing four males had passed through her toll booth and the vehicle was northbound on the thruway. Troop T Trooper Harry Overbaugh on patrol and parked at a crossover near the Saugerties exit, heard the radio alert and while he was listening to it, a Maroon Ford sedan passed his location. He pulled onto the highway, started following the Ford and keyed his radio transmitter: "Kingston, this is 269, I am presently following the suspect vehicle north on the thruway and we just passed milepost 101, what are the occupants wanted for?"

Troop T dispatch replied, "It has not been confirmed but the occupants of the vehicle may be associated with the explosion and destruction of a utility truck. We have also been notified that multiple explosions damaged the main power authority transmission line that provides electricity to the downstate region. The occupants may have some connection. Use caution and do not attempt to stop the vehicle until backup units can assist you. Other units are on their way to assist."

Overbaugh acknowledged the transmission and continued following the Ford, which was maintaining the speed limit and staying in the right driving lane. As the vehicles approached the Catskill exit, the driver of the Ford, activated his right turn signal to indicate he was exiting. Upon observing two State Police cars blocking the exit, the driver of the Ford, veered back onto the Thruway and started speeding up. Four state police cruisers were now in pursuit with blue lights activated. The driver of the Ford made no attempt to stop, instead speeding up and the chase was on. As the chase began, Overbaugh keyed his radio, and transmitted "Dispatch, this is 269, Signal 30. Four units are presently in pursuit of suspect vehicle which refuses to stop." (Signal 30 was the radio code to be used in emergency situations. A signal 30 would cause police units to converge on the endangered officer's location to assist in ending the emergency)

The Ford was fast, but it was no match for the high performance Chevrolet Camaro, State Police cruiser driven by 10-year state police veteran Harry Overbaugh.

"He's doing over a hundred," Overbaugh shouted over his radio. "Cars are being forced off the road. I am going to pull alongside and give him a tap."

"Harry, be careful," Trooper Les Cross, following behind Overbaugh, shouted over his radio in return. Excitement and pumped up adrenalin cast radio protocol aside as he added, "These assholes may have guns!"

Trooper Cross's warning was immediately followed by the sound of a salvo of gunshots. Radio silence had been ordered by troop communications following Overbaugh's signal 30 transmission, and virtually every member of Troop T was pumped up and monitoring their radio receiver. The sound of gunfire raised the tension level and without being ordered to do so, units from as far as 200 miles away started racing to assist their Brother trooper.

In a voice fraught with tension, Overbaugh excitedly transmitted, "They've rolled down their windows and are shooting at me. "I'm going to ram the bastards!"

"Harry, negative," a recognized voice of authority ordered! The voice was that of Troop T Commander Major Harold Sykes. I am dispatching a helicopter with a marksman on board. We are also establishing a roadblock near the Coxsackie interchange. Drop back to a safe distance and keep the shooter's vehicle in sight. Acknowledge 269 and other units in pursuit!"

The four troopers pursuing the Ford, acknowledged the Major's order, by transmitting their unit number and shield. Overbaugh added, "I am behind the subjects now. They have smashed out the rear window and are continuing to fire at us."

Major Sykes responded, "Stay back and just keep them in sight. We have commandeered a tractor-trailer to set up a road block just south of the exit for the Coxsackie rest area pull off. They will encounter the block after rounding the sweeping curve just before the exit. Units are in place and waiting."

Adrenalin pumping and sweating profusely, Overbaugh responded, "Yes sir! Be advised, I don't believe the 'mutt's' in that car will surrender and will go down shooting."

"The road block detail anticipates force Trooper, and they

are prepared to deal with it. All units pursuing the suspects are advised to stop before rounding the curve to avoid being struck by friendly fire. Then stop all northbound traffic, so as not to put them at risk. Hold all traffic until I give you all clear. In anticipation of a lengthy closing of this section of the northbound lanes, after I give the all clear, you will direct northbound traffic to use a crossover, return to the Catskill exit and proceed north on Route 9. All units acknowledge."

Overbaugh and his companions dutifully responded.

Committed jihad soldiers, Mustafa il-Fasid, Narya Bashemi, Ramad Gasmin, and Lemaya Muhammad, would not even consider surrendering to despicable infidels. They would go down fighting, determined to kill as many of the hated American police officers as possible. As all of their explosives had been expended on taking down utility towers and destroying the utility truck, their only armament consisted of firearms. Mustafa possessed the only MP3 machinegun. The others were armed with .45 semi-automatic pistols.

Ramad was driving the Ford and upon rounding a sweeping curve, his eyes opened wide and his body commenced shaking. A tractor-trailer blocked both lanes of the highway and a field of flashing blue lights atop police cars surrounded the truck. Having only seconds to decide a course of action, Ramad swerved off the highway and onto the sloping median. It proved to be a bad mistake. The gently sloped median was soft and mushy. When the speeding vehicle's tires came in contact with the soft turf, it was as if some unseen force had grabbed hold of the car. It flipped end over end several times before coming to a stop; lying with crushed, flattened roof against the ground and wheels spinning in the air. As a result of broken necks and multiple body injury, Ramad and Mustafa died instantly. Both seriously injured, Narya and Lemaya, crawled from the wreckage and commenced firing wildly in the direction of the police vehicles. They were answered by a hail of gunfire. All four jihadists were sent to their dreamed of paradise.

During subsequent de-briefing, Major Sykes commended Overbaugh and all participants in the criminal drama for their professionalism, and how relieved he was that no member of the State Police, or the public had been injured in the terrorist's murderous rampage. Dairy farmer Larry Heath was subsequently feted at a dinner in his honor and presented a "Distinguished Citizen" award.

15

Tom was in his office at the Plattsburgh station when the news concerning the power outage was received. Upon learning the outage was the result of sabotage, via use of explosives, he immediately suspected Omar Bashoul, as being responsible. "That bastard," he said aloud! He then entered the BCI squad room and directed Red Whalen to contact Power Authority Security to find out what happened and the description of any suspects.

In a matter of moments, Whalen re-appeared in Tom's office and advised he didn't need to contact the Power Authority to find those answers. He reported, "Boss, front desk advises that Troop T troopers are presently pursuing the suspects who took down the towers. A 'signal 30' has been called and apparently the scumbags are shooting at the 'troops.' I wish we could listen to the action via radio, but we don't have capability to monitor Troop T radio. We can surf TV stations to see if any of the media has jumped on it?"

It was a well known fact that most major media sources, both visual and print, routinely monitored police frequencies with scanners. Tom, Red and Sergeant Melanie Gibbs, went into the station coffee room and turned on the television set that was positioned on the wall. Local news Channel 5, was reporting that a large segment of downstate New York was without electrical power due to sabotage of 'Nine Mile Two' electric transmission lines. Susan James reported, "Channel 5 has learned that state police thruway troopers are presently in pursuit of the suspect saboteurs. The power outage has caused chaos in the metropolitan area and news affiliates there are presently able to remain on the air via the use of emergency generators. Stay tuned for further details."

Sergeant Gibbs hit the remote button and switched to Fox News which had a helicopter in the air with cameras zeroed in on a group of marked state police units pursuing a maroon Ford sedan. Newscaster Brian Cassidy was reporting, "New York troopers are presently in pursuit of a maroon Ford, which contains subjects suspected of being responsible for planting explosives on electric transmission line towers that send electricity to the New York Metropolitan area from the Nine Mile Two nuclear generating station at Oswego. We have received information that several towers were destroyed and that millions of residents and many businesses in the downstate area are presently in the dark. Fox News is able to broadcast using emergency generators. Approximately one-half hour ago, we received information" (over police scanners) "that a resident just outside of the City of Kingston, in Ulster County New York, contacted police and reported observing the explosion of a utility truck parked in a roadside rest area. This same individual reported the subjects suspected of destroying the truck, left the rest area in a Maroon Ford. Fox news learned" (police radio scanner) "that a Trooper patrolling the Thruway, just north of Kingston, New York, spotted a Maroon Ford sedan containing several subjects and commenced pursuit. The Ford driver is apparently refusing to stop and is travelling north at a high rate of speed. Fox News has just learned that the occupants of the Ford are armed with weapons and have commenced shooting at pursuing troopers. This real life drama is endangering other motorists on the busy New York Thruway."

While the drama was playing out Fox did not move to station break or air advertising.

Tom, Melanie and Red watched in silence as the chase continued. Finally, Tom muttered, "Wonder how they plan to stop these assholes?"

"Yeah," Melanie responded. "I just hope none of our 'guys' get hurt." As she finished speaking, the camera zeroed in on a tractor-trailer blocking the road and the truck was surrounded by troop cars.

Cassidy excitedly announced, "It appears the pursuit is about to come to an end. Oh my! The Ford left the highway and is turning end-over-end. The vehicle just came to a stop on its roof! I don't know how the occupants of the car could have survived that ordeal. Wait, shots are being fired. Apparently, the vehicle's occupants – or at least some of them – did survive and are engaging the police in a gun battle." After a long silent pause, Cassidy stated, "Ladies and gentlemen, Fox has just learned that there were four suspects in the Ford and they are all deceased. The area is presently being sealed off and northbound traffic on the thruway is being re-routed. As more details are learned, we will return to the air."

"Hooray," Melanie shouted! "It appears they took out the assholes without any of 'our folks,' getting injured."

"Yes, thank you God," Tom echoed in response. "I am betting that those four all have Muslim names, hail from Montreal, and were engaged in Bashoul's bidding. Never in my career have I dealt with an individual more diabolically evil than that son-of-a-bitch! What possible satisfaction did he derive from knocking out the power to millions of people, knowing that the power would be restored?"

"You answered your own question Boss," Red Whalen replied. "He is diabolical and probably is presently laughing at all the chaos he caused. I would not imagine he cares one iota that the devoted imbeciles he employed to carry out the plot have been killed."

"You are right Red," Tom answered. "The asshole has all of his rag head followers convinced that if they die in the war against infidels, they will be instantly awarded with a paradise providing them – what is it – 72 or 76 virgins. To believe such nonsense means that obviously they do not have enough intelligence to think for themselves. My concern now is, what new evil plan Bashoul has in the works. We have got to find him and put an end to his shenanigans."

A subsequent Fox News report provided that the four deceased occupants of the Ford, who were suspects in the bombing of the electric towers, "have been indentified, as residents of Montreal, Canada. The New York State Police and FBI are continuing investigation to determine their motivation for destroying the transmission towers and putting much of the New York metropolitan area in the dark. State Police sources believe this was an act of Islamic terrorism, in continuation of Al Qaeda's war on America. An FBI spokesperson, told Fox News that as they had not actively participated in the effort to apprehend the suspects, they were not ready to attribute the power outage to an act of terrorism."

As Tom watched the broadcast, he found it difficult to believe that the FBI was reluctant to refer to the destruction of the towers as an act of sabotage and did not attribute the bombings to an act of terrorism. He swore under his breath when Assistant FBI Director Towson appeared on Fox News and replied to Cassidy's question asking if the destruction of the towers and power disruption was associated with terrorists, replied, "It is highly unlikely."

As he continued watching, New York' Governor Bickford Roberts, asked that residents affected by the outage remain calm and if any sort of special assistance was needed, they could call a special number, which he provided, and they would receive help.

Governor Roberts was followed by New York Power Authority Chairperson Gerald Brown, who explained that every available utility worker was called in and they would be working around the clock to restore power.

Tom stared open mouthed while watching the television screen and shook his head in disbelief as to what he had heard, but mainly his negativity was in regards to what he had not heard. Not one of the person's in positions of authority attributed the power outage caused by taking down transmission towers with explosives to terrorism. *I have to believe they know full well it was an act of terrorism and don't want to spook the public. I would call the FBI to suggest Bashoul is behind this, but would probably just get frustrated and angry by their response if I did.*

The New Hampshire cabin was not affected by the electrical outage, and Bashoul was watching the same Channel 5 news 'special report' concerning the 'sabotage' of the Indian Point power lines. There was a marked contrast in his reaction, as compared to Tom Weston's, except Abdul was disappointed that none of those interviewed by the media attributed the sabotage to Al Qaida, or Islamic terrorists. He was pleased in learning that apparently Mustafa, Narya, Ramad and Lemaya, had performed well. Thousands of American infidels were now confused and probably frightened. He smiled while envisioning the havoc and panic thousands of infidels were experiencing. *This should keep the authorities busy for a while and it is far from over infidels! While you are reeling from anger and shock, Bashoul has another surprise for you.*

16

T om was frustrated and angry. Knowing that anger was an emotion that interferes with and overpowers rational thinking, he tried to stay focused on what more could be done to locate Bashoul. Bashoul had been tricked before by false news and a 'sting' operation. *We need to find some way to inflate his already giant ego, perhaps by causing him to believe he is invincible. I need another fake news story.* He lifted the phone on his desk and called Scott McCormick. His call was answered by the voice mail message: "you have reached the phone of Sergeant Scott McCormick. Scott is presently unavailable as he is chasing butterflies. Please leave your name and number and Scott will either return your call, or erase your message. Have a wonderful day."

"Scott, this is that hemorrhoid New York State Police guy calling. I love your phone message. Wonder how your superiors respond when they hear it. I hope you don't erase me. I've got another request of you. Hope to talk soon, curious as to how many butterflies you captured."

Fifteen minutes later, Tom's desk phone rang. Upon answering he was greeted by a familiar voice, "I just love butterflies. They are so beautiful and so graceful. Hello, Hemorrhoid. Truth is, you are not a hemorrhoid. We are working toward the same goal, and, as a matter-of-fact, you solved a difficult double homicide for us. I owe you Yank!"

"Scott, my brain has been in overdrive trying to come up with a plan to outwit Bashoul. Have you interviewed Jazine yet?"

"No, we haven't. I am confident she will jerk our chain and then tip off Bashoul that we are pestering her. I have been considering putting a tail on her to see if she takes us to one of Bashoul's cutthroats. We have been monitoring Bashoul's cell to no avail. As clever as he is, he has to know it would be easy to trace his whereabouts via his cell. As he is not using his phone and still managing to create havoc, he must be using personal messenger. We know his 'lady love' is operating his store, and she may be handling his evil enterprise as well. Have you considered reaching out to Jason Black? Jason was instrumental in introducing us. He had an excellent police career and has a lot of contacts. He might have an idea that would aid in stringing up – ah, excuse my Freudian slip – capturing Bashoul."

"Jason enjoyed an excellent police career, taught me a lot and we remain good friends. He now keeps busy as a PI (private investigator) and spends his leisure time writing books and painting landscapes. I would call on Jason for advice, but when we last spoke, just the day before Bashoul's escape from jail, he and Patty were headed off on a two-week cruise. I don't want to bother him while he is enjoying a vacation. By the way, I don't know if I told you, I have three of Jason's lovely paintings hanging in my home. Have you seen any of his artwork?"

"That I have mate. Jason presented me with an excellent portrayal of Canadian wilderness. He painted the landscape from memory after he and Patty, joined Michelle and I on a vacation to Alberta. That was a long time ago, while he was still in the state police. We have that painting hanging above our fireplace and whenever I look at it, I recall that relaxing escape from the impossible task of trying to rid Canada of crime. I have also read all of his 'Adirondack Detective' series of books and enjoyed them. Jason was a talented policeman and is quite a talented artist.

As for Jazine, she is somewhat of an enigma. She is a lovely young woman, uniquely possessing probing dark brown eyes that seem to be reading your mind. She is probably quite intelligent and I believe trying to obtain information from her about Bashoul, would be futile. However, if you want us to try, we will go for it. Otherwise, I will assign a tail on her and see if she leads us to her Imam, lover boy."

"We think alike Scott, and are on the same page. I was going to suggest assigning 'hounds' to her."

"We will Tom, and you might be interested in learning that I spoke with Lisha Ishmani, the young lady Angus Horban violated. She is very angry with Imam Bashoul for sending her to Angus. Though angry, she fears Bashoul's power. She claims not to know the identity of any jihadists; however, I've got a feeling she either does or at least's suspects who they are. She did share a very interesting tidbit of information, apparently believing it would not come back to haunt her. Seems Imam Omar Bashoul, believes Allah, directs his life and has given him some sort of superior power. She told me that Bashoul has a special Koran, which has a gem embedded in its cover. He informed devoted followers that this Koran was given to him by his father, who had received it from his grandfather."

"Hmm, interesting," Tom replied. "As he did not have that Koran in jail, I wonder where it is. It is not believed he returned to Montreal after busting out of jail, so where is this precious book of his?"

"I might be able to convince one of our young, dark complexion Mounties to shadow Jazine, and consider temporarily becoming a Muslim. It would be most interesting to learn if something other than prayer is occurring at the Khalil Mosque."

"That is a wonderful idea Scott, but caution your man as to how dangerous it would be if he was 'made' by any of Bashoul's bad guys."

"I know my good man, and that is why I am going to ask Corporal Maurice Longet, if he is up for it. Maurice is very French but could easily pass himself off as a Muslim. And, Maurice previously impersonated a Muslim when we were investigating the illegal sale of young women to men of means. Maurice was used effectively in identifying two of our cabinet ministers as procurers of women. Of course you are familiar with that situation. Haughty Minister of Justice Horban, became a weak kneed coward when we confronted him and played a magnificent role in aiding the arrest of Bashoul. Though rich and powerful, he was not able to prevent Bashoul from rewarding him for his treachery."

"Using Maurice would be greatly appreciated Scott. Let's hope he sees, or learns something that will help move our investigation forward. I will be eager to hear back from you."

"And Tom, I trust that if anything pops on your side of the border, you will give me a shout."

"Of course Scott, keep your fingers crossed and I will likewise. Eventually Bashoul will make a mistake. Good luck and God Bless!"

17

One evening, as Omar sat holding the phone that he dared not use and which was turned off a diabolical plot began to take shape in his mind. It involved his cell phone.

Omar Bashoul's angry outburst in the court room on September 10 had caused the FBI, on September 11, to assign an agent having specialization in telephone and computer technology to attempt trace of telephone or computer communications from his telephone or computer. Three weeks had passed since Bashoul's escape from jail, and SA George Carlin, assigned that task, was bored. It appeared Bashoul was carefully avoiding using any electronic means of communication. Suddenly early one evening, Carlin's ear phones came alive with a voice speaking in – what would later be determined as Arabic. Bashoul was on his cell phone and conversing with a woman. The call was traced to a cell tower on Blue Mountain in the Adirondack Mountains. Subsequent translation revealed Bashoul was conversing with Jazine. He asked her if all was well and if any police had questioned her. Jazine replied that a Royal Canadian Mounted Police Sergeant had come to the store and asked her if she knew where Abdul was - or how to get in touch with 'him.'

"I told the truth Omar. I do not know where you are and could not reach you because your phone was off."

Abdul praised her perseverance, told her how much he missed her and assured her they would be together again soon.

The call was brief; however, Agent Carlin was able to lock in via GPS equipment to the location the call was being made from. It was a remote cabin on Blue Mountain Lake in the Adirondack Mountains.

"We've located him," Carlin excitedly reported to his boss, Assistant FBI Director William Duncan. "He's holed up in a rental cabin at Blue Mountain Lake. He made a mistake and called his girl friend in Montreal."

"Good work George," Duncan responded, "but are you positive?"

"Well boss, just to make sure, I ran a voice comparison and recognition analysis from the tape that Ray Forrest made when Bashoul was arrested. I'm one-hundred percent positive it was him on the phone. Though I'm not sure if it was his lady love on the other end because we don't have preview on her."

"Do you have the cabin pinpointed?"

"Yes sir! It is located on the north shore of Blue Mountain Lake. I identified it as the fourth cabin from entrance of the property that is owned by Harold Gershon. On line the property is listed as 'Leisure Time Cabin Rentals on Beautiful Blue Mountain Lake.' Owner is Harold Gershon, who is a lawyer and resides in Albany, New York. I spoke with Gershon and was told the cabin was rented on line via a credit card – for a period of three months. Card issued in the name of Asgib il-Sashin. Our check with the credit card company reveals Asgib il-Sashin is a 28 year old resident of Montreal, Canada. He is a native of Lebanon and entered Canada in 1998 on a visa to attend an engineering program at McGill University. We did not contact McGill, as leery he might have a contact there who would tip him off that the FBI were inquiring about him. Ask yourself boss, why would a 28 year old foreign, probably Muslim, college student, rent a cabin in a remote region of the Adirondacks?"

"Did you obtain the date of the rental agreement?"

"Yes, and that is somewhat puzzling. The contact for rental was only a week ago. So if Bashoul is in that cabin, where has he been since escaping from jail?"

"My guess is, he has been staying in other locations rented by his 'soldiers.' Did you look for any other rentals by this Asgib il-(whatever)?"

"Yes. Before contacting you, I wanted to make sure we covered all bases. That credit card was not used for any other rentals, and we didn't find any other credit cards issued in Asgib's name."

"Hmm, as the cabin is rented in the name of a Muslim who hails from Montreal and Abdul used his phone while in that cabin, I would say it is safe to say that Bashoul is holed up in the cabin. I am going to put an assault team together and we'll take him down. George, keep listening for anymore calls."

"Yes sir! If I hear anything, I will let you know immediately."

William "Bill" Duncan had been in the FBI for 18-years. He had joined shortly after graduating from law school and passing the New York bar exam on his first try. At 5'10" and weighing 170 pounds, he was not physically imposing, nor was he considered a handsome man. Only 45-years of age, he was prematurely grey, had a receding hairline, a rather bulbous nose and small ears. Duncan had not earned promotion to the position of Assistant Director via good looks, but for possessing a sharp intellect and in stressful situations, he remained calm, cool and in control.

After reporting to Assistant Director Duncan, SA Carlin contacted NASA and asked that when their surveillance satellite passed over the Blue Mountain Lake area of the Adirondacks, they zero in and zoom in on the Gershon property and provide photos. It was necessary for him to explain in detail why this special surveillance was needed as such surveillance was confidential and costly. The official he spoke with eventually agreed to cooperate and advised a close up of the property would be provided within 24-hours.

Upon conclusion of his conversation with Agent Carlin, Duncan contacted SA Harold Thompson, supervisor of the FBI office in Albany, New York; reported that Bashoul had apparently been located in the North Country of New York and directed that agents from that office, in conjunction with the ATF, 'hit' the cabin where Bashoul was believed to be holed up.

Agent Thompson replied that he would organize an assault on the cabin A.S.A.P. After receiving the directive from his supervisor, Thompson called the ATF office in Albany. He explained his plan and advised that as Blue Mountain Lake was in Hamilton County, he planned to have the Hamilton County Sheriff's Department serve as command post for the assault force. He had already contacted Hamilton County Sheriff Ted Munroe, who agreed that his office would host the strike force. Upon conclusion of his conversation with the FBI, Sheriff Munroe was eager for the notoriety that would perhaps inspire a boost in his department's budget.

Harold Thompson, was 55-years old and on the cusp of retirement from the FBI. He was an avid fisherman and had convinced his wife that the weather and sport fishing on Florida's west coast would provide many years of happy bliss. The affable, easy-going agent had never been involved in any shoot out cases. During his long career, he generally worked on solving crimes concerning forgery and fraud, and he counted his blessings for never having had to use his gun. Harold enjoyed biking and hiking and those hobbies kept him trim and in good physical condition. Having a trim physique, the only give-away as to his age, was the 'salt' as he referred to it, in his otherwise dark, wavy hair. Upon concluding his conversation with the Assistant Director, he sat at his desk pondering the forthcoming raid, rubbing his youthful looking chin as he did so. *Hmm, Forrest and Watkins are most familiar with Omar Bashoul, as they worked with the state police to arrest him on the murder charge he faces.* He called SA Ray Forrest into his office. SA Susan Watkins was on vacation.

"Ray, I just got off the phone with AD Duncan. Our intelligence gurus have located Bashoul. Seems he is holed up in a rental cabin at Blue Mountain Lake. We have been ordered to hit the cabin and as you are most familiar with Bashoul, I would like you to lead the raid.

I contacted the ATF and they are going to send four agents. As the cabin is in Hamilton County, I also called Sheriff Munroe and invited him along. He has agreed to let us use his office in Lake Pleasant as a command post. You can select ten agents from this office and I want everyone to stay safe. I understand Bashoul's cutthroats are known to use machineguns and explosives, so utmost caution must be used. Is there any special equipment you would like to take, or anyone else that needs to be called?"

"I am honored that you want me to lead the assault boss. I will put out the word that body armor is to be worn. I would suggest we take a grenade launcher and tear gas grenades. I do think as a matter of protocol, that we invite the state police along. Do you want me to call them, or will you make that call?"

"I'll call Troop B Headquarters right now Ray. Listen in as I make the call and then I will turn the phone over to you and you can discuss arrangements." Using his desk phone, Thompson called Troop B headquarters and connected with Major Chris O'Neill. Major O'Neill was cordial, advised he appreciated being invited to tag along and would provide a contingent of Troopers, which would include the Sergeant-in-charge of the troop's demolition team. Thompson requested all participants in the operation meet at 5 a.m. the following morning, then he turned the phone over to Forrest, who described in detail the raid plan.

Upon concluding his conversation with SA Forrest, Major O'Neill called Senior Investigator Tom Weston. When Weston answered he said cheerily, "Tom, I just received some good news. The FBI has located Bashoul. He is holed up in a cabin at Blue Mountain Lake. Apparently he never left our troop area. A detail is being put together to 'hit' him tomorrow morning at 6 a.m. I am assigning Sergeant Steve Ransom and a couple of 'uniforms' to participate, and thought you might want to tag along."

"I definitely do; however, I've got to ask, are they sure? You know sir, Bashoul is very clever and cagey. Do you know how they located him?"

"I was told he made a call from his cell phone and they got a lock on its location. I was also told they did a voice verification test and it was definitely Bashoul. It stands to reason that he would chose a cabin in our mountains to hole up in, thinking we would be focused on him going to Canada, or trying to leave the United States. Anyway, we – and I will be there – will tag along and hope this puts an end to all of his evil."

"Yes sir. I will see you in the morning."

Upon conclusion of his conversation with Major O'Neill, Tom met with his squad and gave them the news. They all wanted to participate in the raid to take Bashoul down. Tom told them they all had been working very hard to apprehend Bashoul, and he understood their wanting to be a part of his take down, but he did not have a good feeling about Bashoul being careless in using his cell phone. He explained, "I believe protecting Jack, and holding down the fort here is a higher priority."

There was some grumbling, but they understood, wished the raid success and when "Wreck" stated he hoped Bashul resisted arrest and was 'offed,' the others all shook their heads in agreement.

At 5 a.m. the following morning, the normally quiet and subdued Hamlet of Lake Pleasant was abuzz with activity. The approximate 50 police officers, consisting of FBI, ATF, state police and sheriff's deputies were crowded into the Hamilton County Sheriff's department. Although Assistant FBI Director Duncan was present, he directed FBI SA Ray Forrest, to provide the briefing to the raiding party because Ray was involved in the original investigation to apprehend Bashoul.

Forrest provided every participant in the raid a bio and photograph of Omar Muhammad Bashoul, aka, Abdul Markesh. As Bashoul's agents were known to use explosives and were armed with machineguns, it was decided that the raiding party would surround the cabin, remaining 50 yards from the building. It was recommended that everyone in the assault team wear their bullet proof vests. Using a bullhorn, Forrest would identify himself and order Bashoul and whoever was with him to come out of the cabin unarmed and with their arms in the air. "Most likely, he will not comply," Forrest added. "I will give him ten minutes to come out and surrender. Again, I am not optimistic he will comply. At the end of ten minutes, ATF Agents Johnson and Malone (he pointed out the two men sporting jackets bearing letters 'ATF', will advance to within 20 yards and fire tear gas into the building. We will load the cabin with gas. When that happens we can expect to come under fire. If they start shooting, Johnson and Malone will blow the front door with grenades. We will then direct fire into the cabin. I know everyone's adrenaline will be pumping then and I do not want anyone charging into the cabin. I repeat! Stay put! Bashoul and his men are believed to be Islamic terrorists, willing to sacrifice their lives in the cause of jihad. We have to believe they have explosives and will detonate them. Everyone on this detail is eager to capture this scumbag, but I reiterate, I don't want any dead heroes! Don't do anything rash! If he doesn't come out, and doesn't blow up the cabin, we can wait him out - any questions?" There were none.

Briefing over a parade of police cars departed Lake Pleasant and headed for Blue Mountain Lake.

Relegated to the role of spectator, Tom stood at the back of the group and listened. He planned to remain in the background throughout the operation.

The caravan of police cars parked alongside the narrow road that accessed the cabins and cottages dotting the north shore of the lake, at a distance from the driveway that accessed the Gershon property. The detail then proceeded on foot. As they approached the Gershon property, Forrest pointed to a cabin having the number 2 painted on its door. The group formed a perimeter surrounding the cabin. At that moment, Trooper Davis Wachtel, who had been assigned to watch the road where the police cars were parked, and which was the only road giving access to the area, reported on his portable radio that a Channel #5 news van had arrived. Apparently some curious resident in the area, or a member of law enforcement, had called them to report something significant was about to happen.

"Damn," Major O'Neill snorted! He ordered, "Trooper, keep them from coming in here. Tell them we will grant them access when it is safe."

"Yes sir," Wachtel responded!

Of course Susan James and her news crew would be able to hear Forrest's command on the bullhorn, but they would have to deal with it.

"Bashoul, this is the FBI," echoed through the forested area. "We have you surrounded! Come out the front door of the cabin with your hands raised, and when outside, drop face down onto the ground!"

His command was greeted by silence.

"Bashoul, I know you can hear me," echoed through the trees! "You have ten seconds to exit the cabin and surrender! If you do not, we will use force and you will be killed!"

"Come in infidels and we will send you to hell," a male shouted in response, from inside the cabin! The threat was followed by a burst of machine gun fire.

Forrest commanded, "Johnson and Malone launch grenades."

The ATF agents fired grenades from a grenade launcher at the door of the cabin. The exploding force not only blew open the door, but a section of the cabin's front wall.

The chatter of a machine gun followed the explosion and Agent Malone fell to the ground. Johnson immediately locked his arms around his partner's chest and dragged him toward the perimeter. Blood gushed from Malone's left leg and though obviously having a serious wound, Malone told Forrest, "I'm okay, take the bastard's out."

Johnson removed the belt from his waist, knelt over his comrade and used the belt as a tourniquet on Malone's leg.

Major O'Neill keyed the portable radio he was holding and ordered, "Tupper Lake, this is Major O'Neill. We have a man down. Have an ambulance with EMT on board respond here ASAP!"

"Yes sir," the voice on the other end immediately answered.

O'Neill did not have to explain where 'here' was, because every station in Troop B was cognizant of the raid.

As his TC made the call for medical assistance, Tom muttered loud enough for others to hear him, "Damned poor planning! Arrangements should have been made to have an ambulance crew assigned to the raid."

O'Neill responded, "I agree Tom, but we weren't asked for our input or opinion. We were only invited to come along."

Forrest heard the Trooper's dissension, but did not respond. Using the bullhorn he barked, "Fill the cabin with gas." Tear gas canisters were launched into the front opening of the cabin.

The response from inside the cabin was loud cursing in Arabic, followed by a voice that screamed in English, "Death to America! Alihu Akbar!"

"Advance slowly," Forrest commanded.

Those officers eager to make 'the collar' and advancing more rapidly than their comrades would regret their eagerness. The premises had been rigged with explosives. The force of the explosion tore logs asunder and sent shrapnel, consisting of pieces of wood, nails and glass through the air. Several members of the assault team were wounded by the shrapnel propelled via force of the blast. Fortunately, none were killed.

His body shaking and mouth agape. Forrest stared at the area where the cabin had stood. It was no more, and all that remained was a pile of rubble! The scene resembled a war zone.

Having remained on the outer perimeter, Major O'Neill, Tom, Sergeant Ransom and two uniform troopers, accompanied by Herkimer County Sheriff Munroe and two of his deputies, were uninjured. They ran to their vehicles, grabbed first aid kits and commenced rendering aid to the wounded. As Major O'Neill rendered aid, he addressed Forrest who seemed to be in a state of shock. "Ray, you can take satisfaction in knowing none of 'our folks' were killed, and Bashoul, and whoever was with him are no more – actually, a fitting end for the monster."

Tom listened to his commander's words spoken to give strength and reassurance to SA Forrest, and thought to himself, *How can we be certain that Bashoul was in that cabin? A careful crime scene investigation will only turn up pieces of bone and flesh.*

To the best of my knowledge Bashoul's DNA is not on file. It is hard for me to imagine that intelligent, clever, son-of-a bitch would use a cell knowing it could be traced. Speaking out loud he said, "Major, I don't think we should be in a rush to close out our investigation. We need to try to identify the human, or humans, that were in that cabin."

O'Neill turned to face Tom and whispered, "I agree. If the FBI chose to close out their case we should not rush to follow suit."

Upon arrival of the ambulance, Susan James and her Channel 5 film crew were allowed access to the area, with the stipulation that they remain outside the yellow crime scene tape that stretched around the pile of debris. The entire horrific drama had played itself out in under an hour. A bright sun now illuminated the area where the cabin once stood. Smoke continued to rise from the field of debris, which covered an almost 200 yard area and was now clearly illuminated. The thump, thump, thump, of helicopters appearing overhead, announced the arrival of several major network news teams. The world was about to be made aware of the FBI raid to capture 'Fugitive terrorist' Omar Bashoul.

SA Forrest was submitting to an 'on scene' interview by the media. He began by praising the performance and bravery of every member of the assault force. His statement was: "early this morning a task force consisting of FBI, and ATF Agents, assisted by the Herkimer County Sheriff's Department and members of the New York State Police, attempted to arrest Clinton County jail escapee, and suspected terrorist, Omar Mohammad Bashoul, who apparently since his escape from jail, was holed up in a cabin here at Blue Mountain Lake. Bashoul refused to submit to arrest and fired numerous machinegun rounds at members of apprehension detail. ATF Agent Thomas Malone was severely wounded by this gunfire. Subsequent to Agent Malone being wounded, 'we' blew out the front door of the cabin and still

Bashoul refused to surrender. 'We' then approached the cabin to effect arrest and Mr. Bashoul, or his agent, detonated explosives. Several members of our assault force received non-life threatening injuries from shrapnel as a result of the destruction of the cabin. Mr. Bashoul and whoever was with him are no more."

As expected, the horde of media 'Piranha' immediately started firing questions at Forrest. He raised his hands, palm outward, to fend off their verbal assault and responded, "I have nothing to add at this time. You will be provided a more in-depth release upon conclusion of our investigation." He then walked under the crime scene tape to escape further verbal assault.

Tom listened as Forrest conducted the interview. Forrest's concluding statement that Bashoul 'was no more' provoked a scowl and raised eye brows. He said to himself, *you better hope so Ray or your career may suddenly go on downhill skids and come to an end.*

Major O'Neill invited Tom and the other members of the state police who participated in the raid to meet him at Troop headquarters in Raybrook, where they would discuss how to proceed with the state police investigation concerning Bashoul's escape and murderous activities. He offered, "I will spring for lunch. I will have the 'First' (Sergeant George Thomas) order a pizza delivery and we'll eat lunch at a business meeting in the conference room."

Tom had great respect for his Troop Commander and was pleased and relieved during the luncheon meeting to learn they were on the same page. It was decided the investigation to capture Bashoul would be left open for the time being and the security details assigned to Weston family members continued.

Major O'Neill opened the meeting by commending everyone on their coolness and professionalism during the raid. "Every one of you performed exactly as instructed and I am thankful that no one was injured." Displaying a minor note of sarcasm, he added,

"Thank God we were only guests in the 'Feeb' debacle. I wonder if their forensic clean up team will be able to establish how many 'Muzzies' were in the cabin and if one of them was Bashoul. I would lay money on the odds that they will claim examination of the human remains positively identified Bashoul as having passed into his fantasy paradise. During my career, I have participated in several raids conducted by the FBI and, or, ATF, and always came away displeased at how they were conducted. Thankful, we didn't have a 'Waco' type incident in our state. Instead of waiting for Koresh to leave the compound and arresting him, they totally underestimated the firepower and determination of the Davidians and fine federal agents lost their lives in the debacle. And, it sickened me to realize innocent women and children met a horrible death."

He might have continued the negative assessment of the feds if not for the fact that Sergeant Thomas entered the room accompanied by a pizza delivery guy loaded down with several pizza boxes.

First Sergeant Thomas flashed a smile at the group and said, "I see that most of you have already 'hit' the coffee pot or soda machine. If you need a refill, I just brewed a fresh pot of coffee and 'the boss' (troop commander), told me he is springing for sodas. Though I wasn't invited along for this morning's party, if you don't mind, I will join you for lunch." The 18-year state police veteran, who physically resembled the Mr. Clean ad character, minus the earring, seated himself at the conference table and popped open a pizza box.

Major O'Neill laughed and said, "Men, you had better dig in before Sergeant 'Georgy-Porgy' eats them all." When not chewing on a slice of pizza, the group discussed various aspects of the morning's raid and everyone agreed when Sergeant Ransom stated, "For the life of me, as the FBI had cause to believe explosives would be rigged in the cabin, why didn't they conduct surveillance of the premises and wait till Bashoul came outside. We sure as hell would have been able to establish his identity when he was thrown to the ground and steel bracelets were applied."

"Common sense is not one of the feds attributes" Tom answered. "The majority of FBI agents I have worked with are fine law enforcement officers, and they are frustrated by the leadership of political hacks, more focused on satisfying the whims of politicians and protecting image, than law enforcement performance."

Several heads nodded in agreement.

"Enough said regarding the FBI," Major O'Neill responded. "Our focus now is on giving the appearance we are downsizing our Bashoul investigation and if he is alive, he will make a mistake. His powerful persona and hatred of infidels will force him to pull another caper. I would guess that if nothing happens for a month, we can accept that he is dead. What are your thoughts Tom?"

"I agree Sir. Bashoul is a diabolical psychopath who envisions himself as invincible. If he is alive, his strong personality will inspire some sort of evil deed. It would be difficult for him to remain silent for more than a month."

"Okay, it is agreed." O'Neill concluded. "We will leave the investigation open for now, and hope and pray that Bashoul is no more. Once again, my thanks to all of you, for your fine performance this morning; if there are no questions, or concerns, this meeting is adjourned."

Liz kept the Weston television on throughout the day, and had watched the interview of FBI SA Ray Forrest. She felt relief as the statement Bashoul was no more, removed the heavy weight that had been crushing her chest. *Thank you God! Perhaps it is now possible we can return to normal life.* The weight returned when Tom arrived home that evening and informed her that security arrangements were to continue for the time being as he was not so sure Bashoul was dead.

18

S cott McCormick called Tom at home during the evening after watching news reports concerning the FBI - led raid to capture Omar Bashoul. "Congratulations Tom," he greeted! "I was quite surprised and pleased, as were most of our meager staff here at RCMP headquarters to learn of Bashoul's demise. Were you invited to go along on the raid?"

"Yes Scott," Tom responded. "Major O'Neill, myself and four of our uniforms; however, it was entirely an FBI show and we were just observers."

"I was sorry to learn that members of the raiding party were wounded. Is every one of those injured expected to recover?"

"The most serious, is ATF Agent Tom Malone, who took a round in the leg, the others were wounded by nails, glass and other shrapnel when the cabin blew up. They should all recover and be able to return to work."

"So, my good man, now that Bashoul is with his virgins, I presume you are going to close your investigation and are not the least bit interested in our work from this end."

"Scott, the FBI stated Bashoul is no more. Whoever was in that cabin was blown to smithereens, and we (State Police), are not so sure Bashoul is dead. At least for now, our investigation remains open. The explosion was so powerful, it reduced the cabin to a pile of debris, and the identity of whomever was in there remains in question. To my knowledge, we do not have a known DNA sample from Bashoul, so until we are certain he is dead, our case remains open. Do you by chance have a sample of his DNA?"

"Not to my knowledge. All we have on file is his fingerprints, which I am sure you do too. Any fingers found intact?"

"I will have to check with the FBI as they are processing the scene. From what I saw, it is doubtful."

"Well, my good man, if you are interested, I have some news for you."

"Of course I'm interested Scott. Lay it on me."

"We believe we know where and how Bashoul's thugs obtained the explosives and machine guns. And, our resident look like a mid-eastern male Mountie, Maurice Longet, who is very French, has been shadowing Bashoul's 'squeeze.' He looks very 'Sheik' in a thobe. Seems she goes to the Mosque for more than devotion and prayer to Allah. Jazine was observed entering the Imam's office – which is normally a no-no for a female – accompanied by a Muslim male. During her last visit, the male exited the office carrying a wooden box. What was in the box is unknown. Longet described the box as about two feet by two feet, and apparently its contents were not heavy, as after exiting the mosque, he handed the box to Jazine. She took the box to Abdul's Specialty Store, or in her quarters located in the rear of the store. Whatever is in that box most likely is the property of Bashoul, as it came out of his office.

Getting back to origin of explosives and weapons, Longet managed to snap a pic when the Muslim male handed the box over to Lisha. We have identified him as Achmed il-Bysona. Bysona is a 28-year old Canadian citizen, who is employed by a Canadian Defense Contractor. The company was utilized to move material from the Moisie military facility to the military base at St. Hubert, when the Moisie base closed. As all employees involved in the transfer of military ordnance had security clearance, sad to say, supervision of the move was lax. I paid a visit to the Commander of St. Hubert, and he ordered an inventory of base magazines. On conclusion of the inventory, the commander was embarrassed. He told me 10 MP3 machine guns are unaccounted for, along with a large quantity of ammunition. He also told me that records pertaining to the quantity of C4 explosives on hand may be inaccurate due to a check out that had been recorded as "quantity used." We have not brought Achmed in for questioning yet and I wanted to touch base with you before we do."

"My goodness, you have been very busy Scott, and as always, your dedication to this case is greatly appreciated. I am most curious as to what is in that box that came out of Bashoul's office. What sort of trouble would an American cop, posing as a burglar be in, if he conducted an illegal search?"

Scott laughed in response then said, "Well it depends on how adept the burglar is to avoid being caught. If he were to get caught, he might use the defense that he was an invited guest of the young lady resident. The worst thing that might happen is, if observed by someone watching over Bashoul's lady love, is getting shot."

"What I'm thinking Scott is if whatever is in that box is extremely important to Bashoul, he might have a miraculous return to life."

"A Sherlock Holmes ploy and if Omar is not with his virgins, the theft of his prized possession would trigger some sort of reaction."

"Far be it for an honest person like myself to consider theft. What I am considering is hiding a tracking device in the box. If the box leaves Jazine, it would be a good bet to believe it is in the possession of Bashoul. Scott, I would suggest that you not pick up Achmed for the time being. It isn't likely he will tell you anything of interest, and if Omar is alive, he could be communicating with him. Though I do believe it would be in our interest to tail Achmed, as he might lead us to Bashoul."

"For the time being, we will have Longet continue his conversion to Islam, and report the results of 'daily prayer.' What else would you like us to do from up here?"

"I won't add any more to your plate Scott. However, be prepared for the possible resurrection of one of Allah's, or rather, one of Satan's disciples."

"Let's hope not Tom. I have had my fill of that demon and would like a return to the idyllic life I was enjoying before Omar Bashoul began his evil shenanigans. I would think you would also like to start enjoying more time with your lovely wife and family."

"We are on the same page my friend. The sooner this is over, the better. I am planning on taking Liz and our kids to Disney World in celebration. I hope I don't have to call you to come bail me out of jail. Let's stay in touch and whoever comes up with something hot first, makes a call."

"Agreed! Good luck, Sherlock!"

19

As Jack had visited Abdul's Specialty Store several times, Tom asked him to travel up to Montreal with him, and wait in the car as he 'called' on Jazine Jala. Patty Hermione and Troy Rasmussen would accompany them.

Tom found a parking place a half block from the store, then waited and watched the premises. At exactly 5 p.m., Jazine turned over the sign hanging on the inside of the door, to indicate the store was closed. At 5:30, they observed Jazine leave the premises and hail a cab.

Tom exited the vehicle and walked toward the store. He was wearing an ear mike that permitted communication with Patty, Troy and Jack, who waited in the car. They would keep watch and let him know if any police showed up or if Jazine was returning. Before attempting entry, Tom checked for security devices. The store was monitored by a security alarm company and as the residence was attached to the store, it was also likely alarmed. After careful examination, he decided that the alarm warning sign was bogus, intended to scare off thieves. His intention was to accomplish what he intended to do as quickly as possible and leave no clue that the premises had been violated. Unfortunately, he did not discover that Bashoul had installed carefully hidden video surveillance equipment. Utilizing lock picking skills learned from years of dealing with professional burglars, Tom quickly gained entry. As soon as he was inside, he scanned the small premises looking for the box described by Scott. Within a matter of a couple of minutes, the light beam of the small flashlight he was carrying, located the box on an open shelf. He breathed a sigh of relief to discover the box was not locked. He lifted the lid, looked inside and saw that the only contents were a Leather covered Koran and it had a Ruby affixed to its cover. He was most appreciative that the interior of the box was lined with velvet, and this find inspired a smile. Tom carefully loosened the velvet in a corner, placed a tiny transmitter against the wood and fastened it with Gorilla Glue. Then he reattached the velvet and secured it with a dot of Gorilla Glue. The entire procedure took less than 15 minutes. Before replacing the box, he asked Patty, to advise if the tracking signal was being received. She responded that it was. He closed the box, returned it to the exact place he found it and left the premises. There would be no sign of forced entry and according to his companions no one passing by had expressed any interest in what was going on. Upon returning to the vehicle, the group headed for home. Tom had already made the decision to return to Canada the following day and provide a tracking receiver to Scott, due to the distance the signal would be traceable.

20

Abdul sat watching television in his New Hampshire cabin, displaying the joy and excitement exhibited by a fan of a football team that was winning the Super Bowl. Loyal Asgib, had performed magnificently, and surely he was presently enjoying paradise. He said to himself, *Imam Bashoul, this exciting suspense you created deserves an Oscar. Now, I can make arrangements to leave this retreat, leave this vile country and will soon embrace Osama again.*

Moosha had followed Omar's script perfectly. He had rented the cabin at Blue Mountain Lake on line, after finding it advertised on a website in the name of "Leisure Time Cabins", after searching Adirondack Vacation Getaways. The cabin was rented with a valid credit card in Asgib's name. Bashoul wanted to purposely rent the cabin in the name of an obvious Muslim to further excite the authorities. Moosha carefully selected Asgib il-Sashin, as Asgib hated Americans and was a committed jihadist.

Using a pocket sized tape recorder, Omar recorded his portion of a telephone conversation intended for the authorities to hear. Then Moosha had Jazine record her portion of the conversation. Moosha then took the two tape recorded conversations to a professional sound studio, where they were merged into one taped conversation. Moosha then gave Bashoul's cell phone and a recorder to play the tape to Asgib. Asgib was also provided the security code to activate the phone. When Asgib arrived at the cabin in Blue Mountain Lake, he turned on Bashoul's cell phone and dialed Jazine's number. She was prepared and did not utter a word after hitting her receive button. The planned deception was magnificent and fooled the FBI.

A day later Ahmed Gasmani, Moosha's courier, delivered the Plattsburgh newspaper to the New Hampshire cabin. Bashoul was excited and pleased to see the story concerning 'his' death occupied the entire front page. The authorities would not be looking for him now and he could make plans to leave the country. He already had a plan in mind and it just needed fine tuning.

Two days later, Ahmed reappeared and what he brought with him caused Bashoul to put his departure plan on hold.

Bashoul was furious as he examined the photographs and he commenced silently cursing in Arabic. *How dare a despised infidel touch his sacred Quran, especially Weston, who had tricked him into getting arrested?* He snarled aloud, "winter is fast approaching Weston and you have a need to take your precious boat out of the lake. That day cannot come soon enough. Your precious *Hav-n-Fun* is no longer fun, but the means of your introduction to infidel hell! In the meantime, perhaps this smug, arrogant, cocky, police infidel needs to endure some pain and suffering." His face displayed a demonic look as he imagined the emotional pain Tom Weston would endure when he learned his precious Aunt had been taken and was going to suffer a cruel fate.

Bashoul gave Ahmed a message for Dr. Moosha. "The box containing my Holy Book has been defiled by that vile American police infidel. Please have Jazine examine it, remove the transmitter that was placed inside, take it to a public toilet and affix it inside one of the stalls. No wait, on second thought, there is a better solution. There is an identical box in my office at the Mosque. Have this box delivered discreetly to Jazine. Disguise it so that anyone watching her will not recognize it as identical to the box containing my Quran. Instruct Jazine to remove my 'Holy Book' from the box defiled by Weston, and place it in the undefiled box. Then have her take the box containing the tracking device to Trudeau International Airport and place it in a secure locker. It is a certainty she will be followed by police and hopefully the transmitting device continues to send a signal to the infidels monitoring it. They will believe my Quran is waiting for pick up by me, and that I intend to depart by plane.

Having written the message for Moosha, Bashoul reviewed his instructions and realizing how brilliant this scam was, smiled, laughed out loud and said aloud, "I will be in Pakistan smoking hashish with Osama before the infidel gendarmes discover the empty box."

21

Helen Weston entered Saint Augustine Church to go to confession. Going to confession was a weekly Saturday afternoon ritual.

Trooper Linda Barnes sat behind the wheel of her state police cruiser, parked in front of the church, waiting for her ward's reappearance. Normally it took no more than ten minutes for the basically sinless Helen to reappear, as very few people were as devoted to their religion as Helen.

As Helen entered, she noticed the church was practically empty. Father LeBarron was sitting in a front pew, hearing confessions face-to-face. This was fine with Helen, because she had high regard for the intelligent, compassionate, kind Friar Tuck in appearance, Franciscan Priest, of French-Canadian heritage. The soft-spoken Father LeBarron, was never critical, and Helen felt at peace when he gave his assurance that she was free of sin and the Heavenly Father loved her. Helen enjoyed the more personal face-to-face confessional conversation, because it seemed more personal, and it was not as ritualistic as the confessional. There was only one other penitent ahead of her, a man, who had entered the church through a side door. She knelt in a pew at a respectable distance to wait her turn. After kneeling, she closed her eyes and commenced praying the 'Hail Mary.' Suddenly, she was grasped from behind and a man's hand covered her mouth to stifle any scream she might make. The hand that covered her mouth held some sort of cloth that smelled like ether. The last thing she saw before losing consciousness was Father LeBarron grappling with the penitent.

Asim il-Kooma had chloroformed Helen, and his brother, Ashar, had chloroformed Father LeBarron. The two men carried Helen out a side door of the church and placed her in the trunk of their vehicle, parked behind the church. Father LeBarron was left unconscious, lying on the floor of the church. As Ashar and Asim departed, they flashed smiles and waved at the Trooper parked in front of the church.

Unknown to Helen Weston, Jack Weston, Tom Weston and Trooper Barnes, Asim had been discreetly watching Helen Weston's movements for two weeks. Dr. Moosha had assigned him this duty and in the event he was challenged by police, he was to kill as many as possible and not be taken alive. Asim gave Moosha his oath that he would not be taken alive. The il-Koomas abduction of Helen Weston had gone off without a hitch. Dr. Moosha and more importantly, Imam Bashoul, would be most pleased.

After waiting twenty minutes for her ward to come out of the church, Trooper Barnes decided to go into the church and see what the holdup was. Upon entering, she gasped and became wide-eyed as she saw Father LeBarron lying on the floor in the center aisle. She drew her weapon and looked about the church for Helen. Realizing that she and Father LeBarron were the only persons in the church, panic took hold of the young Trooper, who realized that she had screwed up. Her body commenced involuntary shaking and thoughts as to what she should do, and what needed to be done, raced through her mind. Trying to recover and act professional, she took a deep breath and rushed to aid Father LeBarron. She was relieved somewhat to discover he was moaning, breathing and had no apparent physical injury. *But, where is Helen? Hopefully the Priest can tell me.* While checking the Priest's pulse, she fired questions at him. "Father, Father, can you hear me? What happened? Are you okay? Where is Helen Weston?" While asking questions, her olfactory senses detected the recognizable odor of chloroform.

Father LeBarron groaned in reply, "Happened so fast. Two men, one attacked me, one attacked Helen. They must have taken her."

Trooper Barnes heart was now pounding in her chest and she was sweating profusely. *Oh my God! I screwed up big time! I will probably be fired! I can only hope and pray that Helen is not killed or injured.*

When it appeared Father LeBarron had fully recovered, she removed a cell phone from her pocket. She opted to use her phone to deliver her message to the station, as she knew the media monitored police radio communications.

Zone Sergeant Melanie Gibbs, entered Tom's office displaying a grim look.

Observing her entry, Tom set aside the report he was reading and asked, "What's wrong Mel? Something happen to your son?"

Shaking her head in the negative, Melanie responded, "Tom, I just got off the phone with Trooper Barnes. The worst that can be imagined has happened. Helen has apparently been grabbed by Omar's thugs."

Tom felt like he had just been sucker punched. Covering his face with his hands, he responded, in a voice choked with emotion, "No! Please, Dear God, No! What happened, Mel? Is Barnes okay?"

Melanie related what she had been told by Trooper Barnes.

Tom shook his head in anger and disbelief. "What in hell! Why wasn't Barnes with Helen in the church?"

"I asked her that question. She told me that Helen routinely went to confession and had suggested it wasn't necessary for Barnes to go in the church with her. Barnes also thought it would be better if she stayed on watch in front of the church. The Trooper is very upset and confused at the moment."

"She should be," Tom snapped in reply. "Where is she now?"

"She is on her way in. I ordered her to return to the station and submit a detailed written report of what happened."

"Did she see anyone or anything that will help us find Helen, and nail the scum who grabbed her?"

"A Priest was also assaulted and perhaps he got a description of the assailants. She is bringing Father LeBarron to the station with her. I will take his statement. Oh, and you are not going to want to hear this, the abductors left a type written note pinned on the Priest's jacket. The note is addressed to you. It says, 'Weston, you are a poisonous infidel! You have incurred the wrath of Allah! Your precious Aunt is going to suffer a most painful death because of you! Allahu Akbar!" After hesitating to observe Tom's reaction, she continued, "Barnes told me that while she was waiting for Helen to come out of church, a car containing two men left the parking lot. They both waved at her as they departed. No other cars entered or left the parking lot while Helen was in the church. She described the car as a black Ford sedan believed to be about five years old."

Other than displaying a look of contempt, Tom did not respond to the note and after Melanie described the car asked, "How about a plate number?"

"She believes it had New York plates, but she didn't get the number. I immediately had Troop Headquarters issue a radio bulletin requesting all patrols and other police agencies stop and search all black Ford sedans. Do you have any other suggestions?"

Tom was unable to hide emotion as he responded, "No Mel, and I am so upset and angry at the moment I can't think straight."

He emphasized his feelings by slamming his fist on his desk and snarling, "You rotten bastard Bashoul! If you harm Helen, I will personally rip your head off!"

Sergeant Gibbs stared wide-eyed upon observing the man, who in their time of working together always kept his cool and was the epitome of a police professional, explode in anger. However, she understood, and replied, "I share your anger Tom! Why do you think 'they' grabbed Helen, and what do you think they intend to do?"

Anger still reflected in Tom's voice as he replied, "He is using Helen to purposely upset and anger me. The asshole is so diabolical that he is convinced snatching someone I love will cause me to become confused and disorganized. Mel, we now have to pray that Helen activates the transponder I gave her and we rescue her before she is harmed."

"I am not much on prayer Tom, but I will do everything in my power to catch these assholes. Forgive me for asking, but why didn't Bashoul come after you personally, or a member of your immediate family?"

"Because he is unaware that I found the explosives that were planted on our boat. He believes that soon I and perhaps my entire family will board our boat and be blown to bits. I thought the decision not to let the media, or public know about that would prevent him from devising another scheme to hurt my family. I was certain that he would try something with Jack, and he did, but I only gave minimal consideration that Helen was at risk. Actually, it was Major O'Neill's idea to assign Helen Trooper security. Our only hope now is that she presses the button on that transponder."

Upon concluding his conversation with Zone Sergeant Gibbs, Tom called Major O'Neill, who advised he was aware of Helen's abduction, having been informed by Sergeant Gibbs. "Obviously you are upset and angry Tom, and so am I. I have ordered an APB and every police agency in northern New York is presently stopping and searching every black Ford sedan. Of course we have to presume that if spotted, the perpetrators will put up a fight. Dealing with these radical rag heads is totally different from dealing with the criminal element we are used to dealing with. It seems every one of Bashoul's followers are totally insane, and believe if they die while killing infidels they will go to some imagined Heaven, where virgins await them. What in hell is it that causes them to be so easily brainwashed?"

Tom responded, "Do you recall my rant concerning Islam and Muhammad following Bashoul's escape from jail?"

"Yes, and though you refer to it as a rant, it was most informative."

"What I didn't explain during that rant, was that Muslims start infusing, or I might say, brainwashing their children with hatred toward non-Muslims at a very young age. By the time they become adults, those who have become zealots devote their energy and their lives to the destruction of non-believers. They are convinced that losing their life in the war against infidels ensures them of eternal bliss in a paradise full of virgins."

"You are amazing, Tom! I do not know how you found the time to bone up on that stuff. What poppycock though. Why would a supposedly loving, compassionate, caring God advocate and promote the murder of innocent human beings, just because they hold to another religion. It doesn't make sense. Obviously these nut jobs have no compassion for diehard Catholics like you and Helen. We have got to hope and pray we start receiving a signal from her transponder soon."

"It is a good bet that Catholics are especially despised by brainwashed zealots and at the top of their list for extermination."

Tom's next call was to Patty Hermione. When she answered, he asked, "Patty, are you still shadowing Jack?"

"Yes, boss," Patty replied. "But it seems bizarre that a state police investigator is guarding an armed sheriff's deputy, and I know why you are calling. Jack is aware that his mother was grabbed. Needless to say, he is extremely upset and an emotional wreck."

"I want you to tell him not to go home tonight. Bring him to my place and he can spend the night with us. You and Troy can take a break."

"Will do, do you want us to join up with him in the morning?"

"No, I will give Sheriff Benson a call and I think he will let Jack hang out with me until this is over."

"Your nephew has been to hell and back, several times this year, and frankly, I don't know how he copes with the stress and keeps trucking along."

"He is a Weston, Patty! He inherited an indomitable will, strength and stamina from his parents, and he was the protégé of Navy Seal Stan LaPierre." While conversing with Investigator Hermione, the incoming call light on his desk phone commenced flashing. "Gotta call coming in Patty. See you later." Switching to take the incoming call, he answered, "Weston."

He immediately recognized the excited voice on the other end. "Tom, your Aunt activated her transponder. Communications has zeroed in on the signal and traced her location. Actually, 'they' didn't take her far. The signal is coming from a scrap yard, car-crushing facility in Ellenburg. You probably are familiar with the place. It goes by the name of 'Rick's Scrap Yard.' I have dispatched Troopers Mark McMullen and Don Pitcher, both expert marksmen and armed with .308 rifles to discreetly engage the suspects. They are aware that if the 'mutts' holding Helen spot them, they will in all likelihood immediately kill Helen and fight to the death. They have been instructed to proceed without using siren or lights, park out of sight of the premises, then proceed on foot, so as not to spook the nut jobs. Both rifles have scopes, so they don't need to get too close. Stay on the line and we will know shortly what the situation is. Hold on, Pitcher is talking to com now."

Tom held the phone to his ear and could hear the ongoing radio conversation. He listened carefully: "We have the premises under surveillance, Sir," a voice stated. "Two subjects, appears they are armed with handguns. One of them is operating a forklift and it appears he is in the process of picking up a 1996 black Ford, to place it in a car crusher. Other subject appears to be standing watch."

"Don't let them crush that car," Major O'Neill ordered! "Take them out!"

Tom's already pounding heart commenced beating faster as he listened and worried.

"Yes sir," the radio voice responded. This was immediately followed by the sound of gunshots.

Silence followed and while holding the phone to his ear Tom commenced praying. The silence was maddening.

The words, "Suspects have been neutralized and we have secured the victim. She appears to be uninjured," triggered elation. "Thank you God" Tom uttered aloud! He then heard Major O'Neill say, "Remain at the scene until the Coroner and Troop Forensic people arrive. Does the victim need medical attention?"

"No sir," Pitcher replied. "She is shaken but uninjured."

O'Neill picked up the phone, "Tom, did you hear the conversation I had with Trooper Pitcher, via radio?"

"Yes sir! Thank you for ordering swift and decisive action. Would you please have my Aunt brought to my home? I know you will want her statement, and I will take it from her."

"After Pitcher and McMullen clear with the Coroner and forensics, I will have them drop Helen at your place." O'Neill added, "We have sent two more of Bashoul's 'mutts' to their perverted heaven. I am hoping he is running out of jihadists."

"I am hoping the same Sir," Tom replied. "He certainly has to be getting frustrated and angry. Hopefully, anger will cause him to get reckless and we'll grab his ass."

"Tom, Trooper Barnes, screwed up royally. I can imagine you are angry and want her punished. I want to share with you that she accepts having messed up and fully expects to be fired. However, I am reluctant to do so. She joined up with Pitcher and McMullen and personally apologized to your Aunt. I spoke with your Aunt by phone and she told me, she had asked Barnes to wait for her outside the church, and she requested that Barnes not be disciplined. I believe the trooper learned a valuable lesson from this ordeal, and the trauma she endured is punishment enough. What say you?"

"I was very angry and upset Major. But Aunt Helen is okay and recalling personal experiences from my past I screwed up a few times too. I was lucky no one lost their life, and I learned valuable lessons in the process. So, I agree. The trauma Barnes endured in this situation is punishment enough."

"Having you agree is important to me Tom, because I don't want to lose your respect."

"Sir, you need not be concerned. I have the highest regard and respect for you. I am grateful to work for a commander who is intelligent, level-headed and considerate of members under his command."

"Thank you Tom, my feelings for you are mutual."

"Sir, I assigned Investigator Martinez to go to 'Rick's Scrap Yard' and assist the troop forensic team. I want to send photos and prints of the 'perps' up to Scott McCormick ASAP. If we can identify them, we may learn they have a connection to Bashoul."

"Good idea, Tom, and I will have Clair run their prints in our system. Who knows, maybe the 'mutts' have been busted in the states. Do you intend to contact the 'Feebs' to see if they still believe Bashoul is dead?"

"No sir. I assume I will hear from them after they see the news. If they don't call, we can presume it is because they are embarrassed. If you approve, I will head home now, because I am sure family members are dealing with a lot of emotion and I want to be there when Helen arrives."

"Good idea Tom. Extend my concern and best wishes to Liz, Helen and Jack."

When Tom arrived home, he was surprised to see his wife and Jack watching the evening news. He alternately embraced each of them and exchanged a kiss with Liz. Earlier, tears had been flowing from Liz's beautiful blue eyes; however, Tom had missed those moments filled with negative emotion. Upon learning Helen had been rescued and was uninjured, the tears disappeared. Though still a somber atmosphere the relieved members of the Weston family now sat with eyes glued on the television screen. Liz and Jack had been watching local Channel #5 news. Tom grabbed the remote and switched to Fox News, switching back to Channel #5, during commercials.

Susan James worked at displaying a solemn look while standing in front of Saint Augustine Church. She reported: "I am presently standing in front of Saint Augustine Catholic Church in Peru, New York. Earlier this afternoon, well known and respected retired school teacher, Helen Weston, a resident of Peru, went to this church to say confession, not anticipating that evil awaited her inside the church. Two men, apparently intent on abducting Mrs. Weston, were in the church. While engaged in prayer, Mrs.

Weston was attacked from behind and rendered unconscious by chloroform. Church Pastor Father Pierre LeBarron was attacked by a second suspect and also overcome by chloroform.

Helen Weston is the widow of Robert Weston, who served in the military and lost his life in Vietnam. She is the mother of Clinton County Sheriff's Deputy Jack Weston, who within the past three months has survived two attempts on his life. Channel #5 has not learned why Mrs. Weston was abducted; whether her abduction has any connection to the attempts on her son's life and a police spokesperson told Channel #5 that no ransom demands were received and the motive for taking Mrs. Weston remains unknown.

The State Police spokesperson told Channel #5 that a person arriving at the church spotted Mrs. Weston being carried from the church and called the State Police in Plattsburgh. Troopers quickly located the abductors vehicle and followed it to 'Rick's Scrap Yard' in Ellenburg. At the scrap yard, the perpetrators were confronted and refused to surrender. During an exchange of gunfire, both abductors were killed. Mrs. Weston was found in the trunk of the perpetrators vehicle, shaken but unharmed.

We will now switch to Channel #5's John Linton who is at 'Rick's Scrap Yard' in Ellenburg. John, what have you learned?"

"Well, Susan, not a whole lot. As viewers can see, I am standing at the entrance to Rick's and behind me is a chaotic scene. Numerous police cars and numerous police officers are blocking off the area. A State Police Sergeant, apparently assigned as media liaison, informed me that after receiving an excellent description of the abductors and the vehicle they were operating, the car was spotted on State Route 9. Troopers gave chase and as they closed in on the suspects, they suddenly drove into Rick's Scrap Yard. After coming to a stop, they exited the Car, both subject's were armed with handguns and commenced shooting at the arresting officers, who immediately returned fire. Both abductors were killed during the exchange. I was informed that at this early stage in the crime scene investigation, the identity of the perpetrators is unknown and their motive for taking Mrs. Weston is unknown. The State Police Sergeant informed me that as of this time, Rick Justain, the owner of the scrap yard is not believed to have any involvement in the abduction and the perpetrators apparently were trying to evade arrest by driving into the premises containing piles of scrap metal. I was informed that subsequent to a scene forensics sweep and Coroner's investigation; as well as debriefing of Mrs. Weston, the media will be provided an in-depth report; switching back to you Susan."

"John, did you learn the identity of the witness who is responsible for a quick resolution of Mrs. Weston's abduction?"

"No, Susan. I was informed that the witness desires to remain anonymous."

"Thank you John. Our viewers may recall that Mrs. Weston's son, Jack, was nearly murdered this past summer in a robbery attempt during which his diving partner, Stan LaPierre was murdered. Jack Weston survived another robbery attempt about two weeks ago, while employed as Manager of Plattsburgh's Subway Store. The two men attempting to rob the store were killed by off duty New York State Troopers who happened to be in the store. Police investigation concerning the murder of Stan LaPierre resulted in the arrest of Omar Bashoul, a Montreal resident, for LaPierre's murder. Bashoul escaped from the Clinton County Jail, about a month ago via an act of wanton violence that took the lives of Sheriff Deputies, William Hoskin and Theodore Hughes; also the lives of Plattsburgh police officers, James Morrow and Jeff Oates. Bashoul disappeared and apparently went into hiding.

Last week Channel #5 learned of police activity in blue Mountain Lake and learned that during a raid on a cabin by members of the Federal Bureau of Investigation, Bashoul died when explosives were detonated in the cabin he had sought refuge in.

Today's abduction of Helen Weston, who is also the Aunt of State Police Senior Investigator Thomas Weston, who led the investigation to apprehend Omar Bashoul, leaves many unanswered and puzzling questions, such as, was Mrs. Weston abducted by associates of Omar Bashoul, as retribution for his death? Channel #5 will be seeking the answer to that question and viewers will be updated as information is received."

When Helen arrived at her nephew's home, Tom turned the television off. Every member of the family took turns greeting Helen with a hug, and tears appeared on some faces once again. However, this time the tears were inspired by relief and joy. Helen seemed unfazed by her ordeal and thanked her nephew for providing her the necklace transponder. After settling in she told of her ordeal, "The last thing I remember while in church, was Father LeBarron struggling or fighting with a young man. When I came to, I was confined in a completely dark, small place. I started to panic because my initial thought was I had been buried alive. Then I realized that whatever I was in was moving and I could hear a motor. I came to the realization I was in the trunk of a car. I felt about for a trunk release and not finding any, I started kicking at the trunk lid. After a short time, the car stopped and I no longer heard its engine running. Then I heard some sort of machine startup and felt the car being raised. Then I heard the sound of gunshots. Then the trunk was opened, and what a wonderful sight. A handsome, young Trooper took my hand and asked me if I was all right. He helped me out of that horrible place and when my feet made contact with the ground and I saw where I was, I started shaking. I felt God's love and knew it was He who brought those Troopers to my rescue, and they performed magnificently. They saved my life and I want to reward them in some fashion. What are their names Tom, and what sort of reward would be acceptable?"

Tom smiled and responded, "Your young heroes are Trooper Mark McMullen and Trooper Don Pitcher. Aunt Helen, they were doing their job and both neither want, nor expect any reward. It is a certainty they will receive commendations from our Troop Commander and Superintendent. If you want to treat them to a free dinner, I am sure it would be most appreciated. Of course Liz and I would like to come too."

Jack was elated that his mother was safe and sound after her ordeal. While holding her in his arms, he whispered, "Do you have any idea how much I love you?"

Her son's quiet testament of love inspired tears. As the tears starting running down her cheeks, she ran her fingers through her son's hair as she whispered in reply, "Oh, my dear Jack, you have suffered so much, and I love you with all my heart. You so resemble your father, and he was taken from me at a young age. Life would be unbearable if I lost you."

Mother and son then clung together in silence, ignoring the wetness of tears.

Tom gave Liz a look which she interpreted, and she said, "Honey, let's go down to the den and check on our 'crew,' Helen and Jack need some time alone."

Tom arose from his chair, wrapped his arms around his Aunt and Nephew, while he explained, "Aunt Helen, Liz has prepared our guest bedroom for you. Jack, you get to enjoy the futon in the den. Goodnight and God Bless, two of my favorite people. Sleep in peace and awaken refreshed to greet the glory of a new day."

Sergeant Lewis had been carefully coached by Major O'Neill. The media was not to be told that the perpetrators were located via a transponder worn by Helen. They were not informed that a

Trooper had been assigned to guard Helen, and was with her at the church. They were misinformed about the suspects refusing to surrender and exchange of gunfire. They were not informed that Omar Bashoul had ordered the abduction, nor of the note found pinned to Father LeBarron. It was decided to let the media and public speculate for the time being and the discrepancies would be cleared up when Bashoul was apprehended. Basically, the same release was provided to every print and visual media outlet. Of course members of the media, including Susan James, were skeptical about several aspects of the release and Sergeant Lewis was hammered with questions, such as, "Is the state police investigating the possibility that this abduction of a member of the Weston family is in retaliation for the death of Omar Bashoul?"

Lewis's response to this question was: "We are presently looking at all sort of possibilities, perhaps when the deceased perpetrators are identified, their motive for abducting Mrs. Weston, will be revealed."

His response was answered by a confusion of many questions fired at him all at once.

Lewis responded by stating, "You can anticipate that when we wrap up our investigation, all of your questions will be answered. I have been informed that our Commander has scheduled another press briefing for 9 a.m. tomorrow morning, at our Plattsburgh office. Now please excuse me folks, have got to get back to finding the answers to your questions." Having said this, Lewis turned his back on the horde of media and ducked under the crime scene tape.

22

Bashoul knew that when Ashar and Asim had completed their gruesome assignment, they would report back to Moosha, in Montreal. Not having direct and personal contact with the brothers, meant he had to rely on televised news reports to learn the success of their mission.

Bashoul, sat on a sofa in the New Hampshire cabin, holding television remote control in hand and channel surfed various news networks, throughout the afternoon. Envisioning the pain and suffering Tom Weston and Jack Weston would endure upon learning their precious Helen had met cruel death via a car-crushing machine, inspired a smile. He told himself, *Omar, you are truly blessed by Allah. He enables you to make fools out of infidels and gives you the ability to crush them.*

As he surfed between various news outlets, he grew agitated and commenced swearing in Arabic, upon learning the Kooma brothers had been killed and Helen Weston rescued. Somehow, the state police had located Ashar and Asim before they were able to dispose of the Weston woman. The Kooma's were two loyal jihadists and with their death, only Moosha, Ahmed and Paschoo were left to continue jihad. It was time for him to leave this despicable nation of infidels. He would make arrangements and accompany Ahmed to Montreal. Besides, he only had one week remaining on his cabin rental.

Bashoul arose at dawn the following morning and following his usual routine, exited the cabin to engage in yoga exercise while enjoying the awakening sun and accompanying music from birds greeting a new day. The sound of an approaching vehicle interrupted his exercise routine. *Excellent! Ahmed is arriving early today and he will be delighted to learn I am returning to Montreal with him.*

Always wary and cautious, Bashoul, entered the cabin and watched from a window, to make certain his visitor was loyal Ahmed. Recognizing Ahmed's black Mazda, he returned outside as the vehicle stopped in front of the cabin. The two men embraced, and Ahmed greeted, "Good morning Great Imam."

Bashoul noted that the normally always ebullient, smiling servant of Allah had a glum look. "Good morning Dear Ahmed," he greeted in reply. "Why the glum face?"

Ahmed turned, reached inside his car and produced the morning edition of The Plattsburgh Press-Republican, saying as he did so, "Great Imam, I regret to inform you the news is not good."

"I know my faithful friend," Bashoul responded. "Ashar and Asim were murdered by police infidels. They were faithful and true warriors of Allah and you can find cheer in knowing they are now enjoying the fruits of paradise. The day will come when we join them and that day will be the decision of Allah. However, if we wish to please Allah, we have much more work to accomplish here on earth. Today, when you return to Montreal, you will return with a passenger. This cabin and the solitude of this forest have provided a comfortable sanctuary for me but, I have decided the time is right for me to depart this nation of infidels."

Besides, the nights are cold and I feel a nip in the air every day. Winter is fast approaching, and my lease on this cabin expires in one week. Allah has instructed me to go and join Osama in

Pakistan. Be not troubled or saddened my loyal Ahmed. You will remain in my heart and in my thoughts. It is the will of Allah that in my absence, you carry on the war here against infidels. It pleases Allah, and Omar, that you carry on as Imam at Khalil. We are confident that your intelligence, charisma and charm will cause faithful followers of the Quran to fill the Mosque with the thunder of prayer. We are also confident that as a revered leader, you will gather many who will swear loyalty to jihad. You, my devoted Brother have earned this privilege and you shall be blessed by Allah."

Displaying a confused and worried look, Ahmed responded, "May Allah, protect you Great Imam! I swear to Allah that I will carry on jihad and rejoice in knowing that one day I will be re-joining you in paradise. However, I must ask Imam, why me and not Doctor Moosha? He is much more intelligent and much more capable than this humble servant."

Bashoul displayed a smile, placed his hand on Ahmed's shoulder and replied, "My dear Ahmed, Doctor Moosha is leaving with me. The Khalil Mosque is in need of a new Imam, and it is the will of Allah that you take my place. You have studied our Quran and there is no other as devoted to the cause of eradicating non-believers as you. 'We' have great faith in your ability to lead the faithful in prayer, teach them the correct interpretation of the Quran, and like sheep, gather them into the army of jihad."

"I am honored Great Imam, and this humble servant will strive to please Allah and you."

"Ahmed, I know you have great respect for Doctor Moosha and he holds you in high regard. With guidance from Allah, I have tricked the law enforcement infidels, and Doctor Moosha has been instrumental in devising this trickery. Doctor Moosha is traveling with me and his companionship ensures safe passage to Pakistan, where we will join Osama and build a great army. Then we will return to America and destroy these infidel dogs."

As these words cleared Bashoul's lips, the sight of a man approaching on foot startled them. An elderly white male having a slim build and dressed in denim waved in greeting as he approached. The man was not carrying a weapon and no weapons were visible. He seemed to be carrying some sort of food dish. "Hello" the man called out. "Sorry if I startled you fellas. I'm Henry Fording. I take care of this property for Mr. Holloman. He only gets up here a couple times each year. He likes to hunt and fish. Been taking care of this place for 'bout five years' ever since I retired from delivering mail. I came over from my place to show appreciation for treating this place kindly. I like to meet the folks who rent the place and find out if they had an enjoyable stay. I hope you fellas like apple pie? Fresh made by Stella Robinson, owner of 'Stella's Diner,' best eating place in town. Is Mr. Brooks inside? I know Mr. Brooks told me I didn't need to come over here, but I thought he might appreciate some apple pie."

Though startled, Bashoul worked at displaying a smile while studying the interloper with his dark eyes. Ahmed focused on his Imam, waiting the order to strike. That order did not come. Bashoul extended his right hand to the man and responded, "I am Doctor Moosha. I am an associate of Gary Brooks, and he requested I do some research for him. I decided to personally deliver the information and" – gesturing toward Ahmed – "Ahmed drove me here."

Henry studied the taller man as they shook hands and asked, "Has Mr. Brooks finished writing the book he was working on?"

Continuing to smile, Bashoul replied, "The story is nearing completion. He is presently in the process of finalizing the ending."

"Congratulations Doc." Fording responded, then, turning his attention to Ahmed, he smiled, extended his right hand and asked, "Hello, Mr. Ahmed, my name is Henry Fording, you are a handsome fella, welcome to New Hampshire?"

Ahmed stared at Fording displaying a look of contempt and folded his arms across his chest. He refused to shake hands with an infidel and he remained silent.

Returning his attention to the man presumed to be Doctor Moosha, Henry stated, "He ain't a very talkative fella, and he don't appear friendly."

The quick witted Bashoul responded, "My friend is a deaf mute and didn't understand."

"Poor fella, I hope he likes apple pie." He continued, "Mr. Brook's lease is good for another week. Will he be able to finish his book by then?"

Bashoul beamed as he responded, "Oh, it will be finished and I assure you that as brilliant as Mr. Brooks is, the conclusion will be quite dramatic."

"Not much of a reader myself, but I will be eager to read his story. What's the title?"

Bashoul displayed a broad smile as he answered, "Hasn't decided on a title yet. He has been toying with titling his novel, 'The Amazing Escape.'" Changing the subject Bashoul stated and asked, "I didn't hear you drive up. Where did you park your vehicle?"

Fording laughed, pointed in an easterly direction and replied, "My place is only about five miles that-away, and I enjoy walking. I also love the peace and quiet of these woods and mountains."

"Do you have a wife?"

"My dear Thelma and I were married fifty-five years. She passed away last year – danged cancer got her – now I am alone." Changing the subject he asked, "Sounds like Mr. Brooks book is a fiction novel. What other kind-a books does he write?"

Still smiling, Bashoul answered, "He is a master at blending truth with fiction."

"Sounds like he is a pretty smart fella; you must be a smart fella too. Are you a medical doctor or one of those doctors of education?"

Bashoul chuckled as he responded, "I am a medical practitioner and my specialty is ridding our planet of a 'specific' disease."

"Wow! What is the name of the disease?"

Toying with his questioner, Bashoul answered, "Misplaced Dementia."

Henry scratched his head and responded, "Hmm, ain't never heard of that stuff. Is there a lot of folks sick with it?"

Shaking his head in the affirmative, Bashoul displayed a serious look as he answered, "Oh yes. As a matter-of-fact it is pandemic on the American continent. My goal is to eradicate the nasty stuff. We are making gradual progress."

"Does 'we' mean you got a team of Doctors working with you?"

"Oh yes, there is a virtual army of doctors dedicated to wiping out the desease and making great personal sacrifice in the process."

"Wow! Well, I wish you luck, and I hope I don't catch that 'stuff.'"

During their vocal exchange Henry intently studied the man be believed was Doctor Moosha. Curiosity caused him to unconsciously rub his chin as he asked, "You know, Doctor, you look familiar, have we met before?"

"I don't believe so" Bashoul replied. "Probably you have me confused with someone else."

"Probably so Doc, I am getting old and sometimes my mind plays tricks on me. Well, I won't take up anymore of your time. I hope you, Mr. Brooks and Mr. Ah, enjoy the pie. No need for Mr. Brooks to contact me when he is ready to go. Tell him to just leave the keys to the cabin under the door mat. It was a pleasure to meet you Doctor. I hope you are successful in getting rid of that dementia stuff."

Displaying his best false smile, Bashoul replied, "I assure you, Mr. Fording, that Gary Brooks has enjoyed his time here. He informed me the peace and quiet permitted him to be most productive. You shall be amply rewarded for surprising us with this wonderful sweet surprise."

As they shook hands, Henry stated, "Tell Mr. Brooks, I hope his book becomes a best seller." He then gave a nod of his head toward Ahmed, and turned away.

When Fording was out of sight, Bashoul instructed Ahmed: "This foolish old infidel must be disposed of. He has probably seen my face on television, or on a reward notice and when he connects the dots and realizes who I am he will go after the reward. Take care of this minor troublesome matter then return for me. When you return, you may not recognize me. I will be ready to leave. Make it appear that the old fool died of natural causes."

Henry Fording's body would not be discovered until property owner Brett Holoman decided to go deer hunting at his property in New Hampshire. Despite the deteriorated condition of Fording's body, it would be determined that his death was homicide by ligature strangulation.

When Ahmed returned to the cabin from his assignment, he was greeted by a clean shaven, stooped old man, walking with the aid of a cane and wearing an eye patch. He had never seen his Imam minus a beard. Mouth agape, he asked, "Imam, is it you?"

"Yes Ahmed," Bashoul replied. "I am pleased that you had difficulty recognizing me. I feel confident the authorities will also be fooled. Did you dispose of the old pie man?"

Ahmed responded in Arabic, "Great Imam, you commanded

and your humble servant obeyed. Mr. Fording is no longer a concern."

"Excellent! We will now depart this infidel owned hovel and join Moosha in Montreal."

When asked to produce identification at the border crossing, Bashoul smiled at the Border crossing officer and produced a passport that identified him as Henri Moreau, a professor at McGill University. Professor Moreau had met Bashoul while visiting King Abdulaziz University in Cairo, Egypt, and became fascinated by the tall Muslim who was fluent in several languages. Professor Moreau was instrumental in facilitating Bashoul's immigration to Canada and they remained social acquaintances. Having retired from McGill, Moreau no longer travelled a lot and was unaware that his passport had been stolen. Bashoul's disguise was an excellent likeness of the photo on the passport.

As the border guard studied the passport, Bashoul flashed him a smile and said in French, "Good morning Monsieur, I wish you a most pleasant day."

The official seemed pleased, smiled in return and responded in French, "Did you enjoy your visit to the 'states' Professor?"

Bashoul responded in French, "A most productive and exhilarating experience Monsieur. I will have much to relate to my students."

Enjoying their exchange, the guard replied, "Attended McGill for a couple of years. Welcome home professor."

The guard recognized Ahmed as being a frequent border crosser, and called him by name before examining his credentials. "Mr. Ramani, you must be Professor Moreau's driver. Your frequent travel across our border had me wondering the purpose of all your travel."

Smiling as he responded, Ahmed replied in English, "I have been relaying study material to Professor Moreau, while he was on a lecture tour in the states. He pays me very well and tries very hard to teach me French, but I am a poor student in that language."

"Well gentlemen," the guard answered in English, "Welcome home!" The barrier gate lifted and Ahmed slowly exited. Driver and passenger, exchanged looks and both uttered sighs of relief. As they proceeded toward Montreal, Bashoul asked, "Ahmed was Doctor Moosha given my instructions?"

"He was, Imam."

"Good! Ahmed, I want you to know how much you are appreciated. You have been and continue to be a trusted warrior of Allah. You please Allah greatly and as previously explained, he wants you to take charge at Khalil and devote yourself to enlisting an army of loyal jihadists to carry on the war against infidels. When I arrive at my destination, you will be contacted and provided financing that will enable you to support 'our' army."

Ahmed responded by touching forehead, lips and breast with his right hand, a Muslim's way of showing respect and appreciation. "I am honored Great Imam! I will strive to please Allah."

23

Tom was in his den channel surfing news programs, when Beethoven's Fur Elise, sounded on his cell phone. As a fan of classical music, especially that of Ludwig Beethoven, he had purchased his favorite, 'Fur Elise' for his ring tone. He recognized the number displayed on his phone's screen as belonging to Scott McCormick.

"Hey Scott," he answered, "apparently, you have been watching the news."

"Aye, that I have Tom. What in the world is going on? It was only a week ago that your FBI informed me Omar Bashoul was no longer walking planet earth. Although your state police sergeant did his best to obfuscate the media, the fact that Mrs. Weston was snatched by goons, tends to make me believe you were right when you told me you suspected that the clever Muslim was alive and had pulled a fast one on your feds. However, the snatching of your Aunt just doesn't make sense. What was 'he' hoping to accomplish by taking a woman that had nothing to do with his situation. The only conclusion I could draw was that Bashoul, though intelligent and clever, is insane as well. I am happy to learn your Aunt was rescued and apparently not harmed. Of course my always suspicious police mind tells me you troopers were not honest and forthright with the media. Am I correct, and if so, are you willing to share more precise information with an inquisitive Mountie?"

"Scott," Tom responded, "you are quite astute. There were details we were not at liberty to share with the public at this time. We did not reveal that the abductors left a note, directed to me, pinned to the Priest's cassock. The note was typewritten and stated that as I had incurred Allah's wrath, my Aunt Helen was going to be sacrificed. That came very close to happening as Bashoul's animals were in the process of placing the car having Helen trapped in its trunk, inside a car crushing machine. We were able to get to her and off the scumbags before they completed their mission because she activated the transponder I provided after Bashoul escaped from jail. The part about the perpetrators engaging in a shoot out was also not true. The crud did not know two Troopers were watching them and when our commander learned the kidnap car was about to be placed into a car crusher, he ordered the troopers to execute the scum. Both troopers are marksmen and they performed magnificently. As yet we haven't identified the perpetrators and if we cannot come up with an id. on them, I will provide their prints and photos to you. It is a 99.9% certainty that they will be identified as Muslim and associates of Omar Bashoul."

"Superb thinking on your part my good man also, smart move to have her provided with a transponder thingy. That note is confusing. How does doing your job as a police officer offend Allah? Also, why didn't he send his thugs after you rather than your Aunt? Frankly, hate filled Muslims are hard to understand."

"In answer to your question Scott, the media and public were not made aware that a bomb had been placed aboard my boat. I believe Bashoul assumes that he will be rid of me the next time I start up my boat. However, I am also puzzled as to what made him so angry that he decided to kill Helen. He definitely

The Twentieth Terrorist

is the personification of evil, and possibly not even human. What possible pleasure could any rational thinking; especially a supposedly religious human being, derive from sadistically destroying a harmless, innocent woman?"

"Could it be he is aware that you broke into Jazine's apartment?"

"As you still have a fix on the bug I placed in his precious Quran box, I don't think so. If he discovered my entry, the first thing he would have done is check his precious box and remove the bug."

"As a matter-of-fact, that is another purpose of my call this evening. The transmitter is still working and Corporal Longet followed Jazine, carrying the precious Koran box to Trudeau Airport. Longet called me all excited because he thought Jazine was going to meet up with Bashoul and they planned to flee by plane. To his surprise, Jazine placed the box in a rental locker – number twenty-six – at the airport, and then returned home. It appears our elusive Imam intends to fly out of Montreal soon and will take his precious box with him. I have assigned Mounties to keep the locker under surveillance. The young Casanova's thanked me for giving them the opportunity to sit on their tails, reading newspapers and ogling lovelies passing by. I reminded them of their purpose in being there and also cautioned them as to the danger they would be in if Bashoul made them."

"Very interesting Scott, it does appear that Bashoul intends to leave by plane. He has to know that his face has been all over every news network and that the reward for information leading to his arrest is now $100,000, so it is a sure bet that he will disguise his identity. Your men must be made aware of that and be on their guard. Do you think he intends to take Jazine with him?"

"My guess, Tom, is that he will. After all, she is his love interest and she has remained very loyal to him. I am hopeful he makes his move soon, because we have committed a lot of manpower to nab his arse, and I expect my Super is going to start complaining about all the 'Looney's' it is costing."

"I have been hell-bent on nabbing his ass here in the states, but that hasn't happened and now it appears it won't happen. There are a large number of police officers down here, including a certain Senior Investigator, who would love to send the demonic bastard to his imagined paradise. Since his escape a month ago, we have had a task force dedicated to capturing him and although we have diminished his number of jihadists, he has proved too clever for us. I must admit Scott I am frustrated, angry and tired. My family is living on pins and needles, constantly worrying about their personal safety and mine. I am also nagged by knowing that when we do find and arrest 'him,' the only punishment he faces for all the murder and mayhem he has committed, is life in prison. If you don't mind Scott, I would like to come up to your bailiwick and be a part of his 'take down.'"

"My good man, when Bashoul was arrested in New York City, you were very gracious in inviting me to be a part of that take down, so you are quite welcome to join us. The problem is, we don't know when he will appear. It could be tomorrow, or a month from tomorrow. What about your Federal government? I would think Bashoul qualifies as a terrorist and if memory serves me correct, there is a death sentence for that."

"Yes, Scott, there is no doubt, nor question, that Bashoul is an Islamic terrorist and had an integral role in the horrendous attack on 9/11. However, the embarrassment of charging a suspect that the FBI has declared dead might cause the Feds to decline prosecution. I will clear travel and expenses with Major O'Neill. If he gives his approval, you can expect me to arrive up there tomorrow. I don't want to miss the action."

"Observing the look on Bashoul's face when he sees his nemesis will be a highlight in my career, and you are welcome to stay at my humble abode while you are up here. That will give us the opportunity to knock down some Guiness, and share war stories."

"Scott, you are kind and your offer is most appreciated. You know, as morbid as it may seem to say so, Bashoul is responsible for one positive thing. His evil shenanigans in the USA and Canada caused our bond of friendship. Be prepared my friend, because after downing two beers I become a boring conversationalist. Most of the crimes I have investigated during my twenty plus years in the State Police were fairly easy to solve and do not merit talking about. I must admit that the asshole we are presently trying to capture, takes the prize for being the most diabolical, most clever, most vicious, criminal I have run across in my career. I am frustrated and tired. I have decided that after this Disciple of Satan is no longer a threat, I am going to pull the plug and retire."

"Likewise my good man, Bashoul ranks at the top of my list too. We also have to thank your former State Police protégé Jason Black, for introducing us. Formerly, my work in our intelligence unit mostly consisted of conducting background investigations on political appointees, and monitoring government official's moral, and ethical behavior. Pretty mundane work compared to what we are involved in now. After you arrive, we will put our graying heads together and come up with a plan to end Bashoul's reign of terror."

24

To passer bys, or perhaps a police surveillance team, the man entering the doctor's office was just another patient. The stooped over, clean shaven elderly man, shuffling along with the aid of a cane, bore absolutely no likeness to the tall, bearded, middle-aged Imam, known as Omar Mohammad Bashoul.

Upon entering the office, the man's appearance immediately changed. Doctor Moosha greeted Omar in Arabic, "as-salam alaykum Imam," translation, "Greetings Imam." They embraced and Bashoul replied, "Wa-Alakum-Salaam Babila Moosha", translation, "And unto you peace dear Moosha." The two men continued conversing in Arabic. Bashoul asked: "Is all ready for our departure?"

"Would I fail you Imam," Moosha replied. "You will be pleased to know that your Quran is safe. I have a very fast boat tied up at the Jacques-Cartier pier. Your Quran is on board. When you are ready, we can depart. I have booked passage on an Iranian freighter which we will board in mid-river, (Saint Lawrence), ten miles from Montreal. The Captain was most accommodating when I offered twenty-thousand Rials for our travel to Iran. After arriving in Iran, it will be a simple matter to find travel to Pakistan."

Bashoul smiled and embraced Moosha again. "Babila Moosha, you are amazing! Your ingenuity and intelligence rival my own.

Osama will be most pleased to see us. My only regret at leaving is being separated from Jazine. She is a beautiful flower and she gives me much pleasure. Has she been given instructions?"

"Yes Imam! Pursuant to your instruction, this afternoon Jazine is going to the airport and will purchase two tickets for flight to London."

Bashoul laughed and clapped his hands in glee. "Wonderful! The purchase of those tickets will excite the authorities watching her. They will believe that I am joining her on the flight to London. I would love to see the look on their faces when she removes the empty box from the locker. Just imagine their dismay when I do not appear and she flies alone. They will undoubtedly have several agents on the plane with her, under the impression she will be meeting me in London. When I do not appear they will take her into custody and open the box. I would love to be there to see their surprise and chagrin when all they find in the box is their nasty device and the note I left them. Of course that is not possible, so I will have to wait for Jazine to relate how they reacted."

Joining his friend in laughter, Moosha replied, "Imam, by the will of Allah, you are truly a genius. You continue to make foolish monkeys out of infidels. I would also like to see their embarrassment when they confront Jazine in London. It was also a work of genius placing the note ridiculing them in the box. They will feel like fools and be very angry. Of course by then they will be powerless to do anything, because we will be halfway to Iran."

When they finished laughing and wiped tears from their eyes, Moosha asked, "When do you wish to depart Imam?"

"Tomorrow, Dear Moosha! Please bring your bag and the one you packed for me and let us be off. If acceptable, I will stay this final night in your office."

"Of course Imam, it pleases me that you have arrived here safely and trust the accommodations of my humble office."

The following morning, Dr. Moosha, holding his disabled patient by the arm, hailed a cab and twenty minutes later they arrived at 'Jacques-Cartier' pier. After exiting the cab, both men stood for a moment studying their surroundings, looking for possible danger. Moosha was armed with a 9mm Beretta and he informed Bashoul that he had placed a 9mm Sig-Sauer under the aft boat cushion. Only two persons were observed within 100 yards of the sleek 19 foot Sea Ray rented by Moosha. The paved travel area of the pier was some 12 feet above the water's surface as the pier was designed to accommodate ocean going vessels. The Sea Ray sat atop the water about 8 feet below the top of the pier. It was secured fore and aft to dock pylons by sturdy lines. Bumpers on the port side of the boat protected the boat from being damaged by incoming wash from ships passing by. A steel rung ladder permanently fixed to the pier permitted access to smaller vessels.

One of the men they observed was dressed in shorts, topped by a loose fitting sweat shirt. He was engaged in polishing the hull of a sleek, triple deck cruiser moored in front of the Sea Ray. The other man, clad in denim, head topped by a beret, was fishing from the pier's edge. Satisfied that they faced no danger, Bashoul nodded to Moosha, preceded Moosha down the ladder and settled on the aft seat of the boat. Moosha commenced untying the bow mooring line, when the man who had been polishing the cruiser suddenly appeared beside him. The man smiled and said, "Nice looking boat. It must be fast. Climb aboard friend, and I will un-tie for you."

Moosha studied the man, decided he presented no danger, and replied, "Thank you."

He descended the ladder, climbed aboard the Sea Ray, and

started its motor. Waiting for the mooring ropes to be untied and thrown down, suddenly, he observed the man who had been fishing, standing beside the other man. He heard this man say, "Here, let me help."

Bashoul eyed the two men with curiosity. They seemed clumsy and slow at untying the lines. The fisherman spoke: "Doctor Moosha, your patient appears to have had a miraculous healing."

Bashoul's eyes opened wide, in recognition of the voice. "Weston! I misjudged your intelligence and ingenuity." While speaking, he slowly reached beneath the seat cushion and grasped the Sig-Sauer semi-automatic, concealed there. He asked, "How did you find us Weston?"

Tom's eyes focused on the monster sitting so calmly below him and his mind filled with angry emotion. *You monster! You have no conscience and take pleasure in ordering the murder of innocent people. Bashoul, you are a vile, despicable human being!* He responded, "Your ego Bashoul! You love to read news about yourself in the newspaper! Thank you Press-Republican!"

Bashoul snarled in response. "So, you have come to arrest me, but you have no authority here Weston!"

Tom smiled, pointed to the man clad in shorts and said, "No, but he does! Meet my friend, Sergeant McCormick, Royal Canadian Mounted Police!"

Bashoul responded by pulling the Sig-Saur from beneath the boat cushion. He commenced firing at his nemesis. Moosha pulled out his Beretta and fired toward the two infidels.

Upon seeing the weapons, Tom and Scott ducked down, so they were out of sight of the boat occupants.

Tom called out, "Hey Bashoul, it gives me great pleasure to expedite your travel to paradise!" He removed the grenade he had been holding onto in his pocket, pulled the pin and dropped it over the edge of the pier.

For the first and final time in his life, Bashoul knew fear. That look of panic and fear disappeared as the grenade struck the deck of the boat.

Moosha had begun shaking with fear upon recognizing the dire predicament he was in and the hand firing the Beretta shook uncontrollably.

Bashoul made an attempt to grab the grenade and throw it overboard; however, he was not quick enough. The grenade exploded in his hand, ripping his body apart and the blast caused the boat's full tank of gasoline to explode. The explosive inferno ripped boat and occupants apart and sent Bashoul's treasured Quran, or what remained of it, floating in the Saint Lawrence River.

25

The following bulletin interrupted CNBC news, to be followed soon after on most major American news networks: "It has been learned that an explosion this afternoon, aboard a boat tied up at Jacques-Cartier Pier, took the lives of the boat's two occupants. It was reported that gunfire was heard in the vicinity just prior to the explosion. Montreal Metropolitan police are presently at the scene and (station identification) is awaiting a police report. Stay tuned for further details."

This bulletin was soon followed by another bulletin, and television cameras zoomed in on the Khalil Mosque in Montreal, as the newscaster announced, "A dramatic shoot out at the Khalil Islamic Mosque this afternoon, between Royal Canadian Mounted Police and suspected Islamic terrorists, police were attempting to arrest, ended in the death of the two suspected terrorists. Authorities report that twenty-seven year old Paschoo Mulalo and twenty-eight year old Ahmed Raman, suspected Al Qaida terrorists, refused to submit to arrest and died during an exchange of gunfire. Inspector Claude Martine, of the RCMP, told your CNBC news team that Mr. Raman and Mr. Mulalo, had been identified as associates of Omar Mohammed Bashoul, former Imam of the Khalil Mosque, who was arrested by American authorities in early September, charged with the murder of an American citizen. On September 21, Imam Bashoul escaped from the Clinton County, New York jail, where he had been incarcerated following his arrest. During the escape, four American police officers were killed. It was subsequently learned that Bashoul had connections to the group of terrorists, who hijacked planes and used them on a suicide mission to kill Americans. American and Canadian police commenced a massive manhunt to locate and re-capture Imam Bashoul. A $100,000 reward had been offered for information leading to his arrest. As previously reported, authorities advised that Imam Bashoul was killed during a raid on his hide-out in the Adirondack Mountains. Inspector Martine told CNBC that police learned that Mssrs. Raman and Mulalo were henchmen for Imam Bashoul. When asked if the shootout at the Mosque was connected to the shooting and explosion at Jacques-Cartier Pier, Martine advised it is not believed so; however, investigation is ongoing."

The Plattsburgh Press-Republican would subsequently report under the headline: 'North Country Reign of Terror Over,' New York State Police Troop B Commander Chris O'Neill, reports that the nearly three-month long investigation to apprehend murderer/ Clinton County Jail escapee Omar Mohammad Bashoul, ended yesterday when Bashoul ignited an explosive device on board a boat he apparently intended to use to flee America. The boat that exploded was tied up at the Jacques-Cartier Pier in Montreal.

The Major explained: originally it was believed that Mr. Bashoul, killed himself during a raid by the FBI on a cabin located in Blue Mountain Lake. As the remains of the deceased could not be positively identified, we decided to leave our investigation open. It is believed that while Mr. Bashoul was on the run, he created diversions to take the authorities focus off of him. Those incidents involved death and destruction and created angst in North Country residents. Following the abduction of Peru resident Helen Weston, we became certain that Bashoul was still alive. Via personal and electronic surveillance on known associates of Bashoul, with the help of members of the Royal Canadian Mounted Police, we were able to locate Mr. Bashoul in Montreal; where he was in the process of trying to flee the American continent by boat. When confronted, rather than submit to arrest, Mr. Bashoul ignited explosives on board the boat.

Bashoul was accompanied on the boat by well known Montreal physician Muhammad Moosha, who was also killed in the explosion. The Doctor's relationship to Mr. Bashoul is unknown.

When asked if Montreal residents Ahmed Raman and Paschoo Mulalo, who were killed by police at the Khalil Mosque in Montreal, during their attempted arrest; were connected to the boat explosion that took the life of Omar Bashoul and Doctor Mohammad Moosha, the Major told the Plattsburgh Press-Republican that the New York State Police were not involved in that incident and therefore he was unable to comment about it.

Chief Constable Pierre Bouvier, of the Quebec Provincial Police, told the Plattsburgh Press-Republican that Canadian authorities had identified Ahmed Raman and Paschoo Mulalo as associates and hit-men for 'suspected' terrorist Imam Bashoul.

When asked if police were positive Imam Bashoul was killed in the explosion, Major O'Neill stated that members of the Royal Canadian Mounted Police, accompanied by New York State Police, were attempting to apprehend Bashoul and made positive identification prior to the explosion.

Major O'Neill praised the Royal Canadian Mounted Police, especially Sergeant Scott McCormick and Corporal Maurice Longet, for their expertise and excellent cooperation, without which Mr. Bashoul, would probably have succeeded in fleeing America. It was also pointed out that the investigation to capture a man responsible for a reign of terror, involved tireless devotion and dedication on the part of many police officers. They are owed great praise and gratitude for their efforts to bring a monster to justice.

O'Neill also extended condolences to the families of the police officers and citizens, who were killed during the reign of terror. O'Neill plans to ask that the reward offered by North Country business community members, be distributed to the spouses of the Clinton County Sheriff's Deputies and Plattsburgh City police officers murdered by Bashoul.

In closing, Major O'Neill expressed his thanks and appreciation to the good citizens of New York, for their patience, perseverance and cooperation during Bashoul's reign of terror. Peace and tranquility are once again hallmarks of the North Country."

What Major O'Neill did not relate, was that all members who labored to catch a terrorist killer, were to be rewarded by a banquet at which, commendations would be awarded.

26

The banquet was held at the magnificent Hilton Inn, located in the Village of Lake Placid, overlooking serene, placid Mirror Lake. Located in the heart of New York's Adirondack Mountains, the Swiss atmosphere village had hosted the 1980 Winter Olympics, and New York State Police Troop B headquarters was located just outside the village.

New York State Police Superintendent Harold Grayson and RCMP Inspector Claude Martine were invited and asked to present commendations to members of their commands.

RCMP Sergeant Scott McCormick accompanied by his wife Michelle; along with Corporal Maurice Longet, accompanied by his fiancée Jeanine; Investigator William "Red" Whalen accompanied by his wife Colleen, joined Tom and Liz Weston at a table.

Patty Hermione, accompanied by Troy Rasmussen; along with Ed Czech and wife Carol, joined Helen and Jack Weston at a nearby table.

Enrico Martinez, accompanied by Trooper Patricia Harmon; joined Ed LaPlante, Enrico Martinez, Bill Whalen and wife Lynn, at another nearby table.

Though attended by a plethora of brass, it had been predetermined that speeches would be short to focus on everyone just relaxing and enjoying the evening. The longest part of the program was the awarding of plaques and certificates to those who worked on the investigation and to the spouses of those who were killed.

Upon arrival at the ceremony, Tom greeted Major O'Neill and asked that he be the last award recipient as he desired to make a special announcement.

While enjoying pre-dinner cocktails and conversation, Red Whalen asked Tom: "Boss, I know you are a whiz at solving crossword puzzles, but I am really curious as to how you managed to assemble the jig-saw puzzle that revealed Bashoul was connected to Moosha and that they were attempting to flee by boat?"

Displaying a leprechaun type of grin Tom replied, "Red, you actually discovered the first piece of the puzzle when you reported that Doctor Moosha had a subscription to the Plattsburgh Press-Republican. That caused me to have Scott take a look at the Doctor. Scott found the rest of the pieces, so I will let him give you those details."

Scott's face exhibited a glow of appreciation for having the honor of completing the story and he intended to make it as dramatic as possible. He pointed to Corporal Maurice Longet, as he began to slowly explain: "Our investigation to capture a monster can be compared to a game of chess. You Yank's and we Mounties were pitted against a Chess Master by the name of Omar Bashoul. Consider Bashoul as King on the board. Jazine Jala was his Queen, Doctor Mohammed Moosha and Ali Raman, were his Knights. His Rooks and Pawns consisted of loyal Islamic jihadists. As you Yank's gradually captured, or rather eradicated, Bashoul's Rooks and Pawns, the Chess Master made a brilliant move which took your FBI out of the game, causing Bashoul to declare 'Check.' However, Tom and you intelligent State boys were not so quick to concede victory. When Tom asked me to take a look at Plattsburgh Press-Republican subscriber Doctor

Moosha, the only link connecting the Doctor to Bashoul was that virtually all of Bashoul's Pawns were patients of the Doctor; that and the fact that as a Muslim, Doctor Moosha was also a member of the Khalil Mosque." Pointing to Corporal Longet, he continued: "This Omar Sharif look alike young Mountie, agreed to temporarily convert to Islam. Maurice commenced shadowing Jazine and later Doctor Moosha. He faithfully attended prayer sessions at the Khalil Mosque. I can imagine that when Maurice made his appearance in the Mosque, many pairs of dark eyes, faces hidden behind nigabs were studying him. Thank goodness he didn't submit to temptation and remained focused on his assignment."

Pausing for a moment to let laughter subside, Scott continued, "It seems incredible that Maurice, who doesn't speak a word of Arabic, was able to be accepted by the Muslim community. He was magnificent! A few days ago, he reported that Jazine, entered the Imam's office at the Mosque, which was believed to be a no-no for women. She was accompanied by Ahmed Raman and he observed them exit the office carrying a box identical to the box that (pointing to Tom) Sherlock here, planted a tracking device in. Maurice tailed Jazine to Doctor Moosha's office. She entered the office carrying the box and exited minus the box. This generated curiosity and suspicion. We already knew that Jazine had placed the box, supposedly containing Bashoul's precious Koran, in a locker at the airport, and Mounties were assigned to watch that locker. The appearance of an identical second box definitely grabbed our attention, so Maurice was asked to focus on Doctor Moosha. He followed Moosha to the Jacques-Cartier Pier and watched Moosha place the box given to him by Jazine, on board a boat tied to the pier. Maurice's work gave us the edge in the chess match, and our King, Tom Weston, was with me in Canada, when Maurice reported his observations. Maurice had also noted the name on the vessel and we traced its ownership to a boat-leasing agency. I contacted the agency and 'walla' the boat had been leased by none other than Doctor Mohammad Moosha. Tom and I decided to continue a large police presence at the airport to give the impression we believed Bashoul intended to fly out of Montreal. It was decided that a low-profile was needed at the pier so as not to spook Moosha. Tom and yours truly took on the roles of fisherman and boat polisher. I don't know why I agreed to take on the labor of waxing a boat, while Tom sat idly on the edge of the pier impersonating a fishing expert. Although, considering He was our King and I was just a Rook, I was relegated to performing as directed. While languishing on the edge of the pier holding a fishing pole that didn't even have a hook attached, King Tom kept casting looks at me and smiling. It was galling!"

This statement inspired another round of laughter causing Scott to pause in telling the outcome of the chess match.

When the laughter subsided he continued, "Of course we were dressed appropriately for our role playing and my weapon that I had in a holster on my belt and worn in the center of my back was irritating. I was under the impression that Tom was wearing his weapon in the same fashion, or perhaps in an ankle holster. Not knowing what to expect, we did not bring any heavy-duty armament – or at least, I was under the impression we hadn't. Doctor Moosha's appearance accompanied by a crippled, stooped over fellow wearing an eye patch, definitely got our attention, and my heart was beating so fast, it was difficult to not display interest. After eyeing us, Moosha's crippled patient, suddenly straightened up, grabbed the top of the pier ladder granting access to the boat and scurried down the ladder. Bashoul had disguised himself magnificently, but at that moment, we had no doubt that the Chess Master had made a very bad move. Tom signaled to me and as Moosha commenced undoing the tether connecting the boat to the pier, I went to him and offered to undo the line. Moosha accepted my offer and descended onto the boat. While I fiddled with the rope, Tom joined me. It was an exhilarating moment and oh, you should have seen the look on Bashoul's face when Tom said, 'Doctor Moosha, it appears your patient has made a miraculous recovery.' Of course we were expecting that whoever showed up to get aboard the boat would be armed, so it was no surprise, when Bashoul and Moosha started shooting at us. As we were above them on the pier, all we had to do was duck down to avoid being hit. The checkmate moment totally surprised not only Bashoul and Moosha, but this Mountie as well." Pausing, Scott turned to Tom and asked, "Do I have your approval to relate the move that ended the game, or does it remain for others to guess?"

Tom smiled and replied, "Let's just say that good won over evil. Whatever caused the explosion sent a Disciple of Satan back to Hades, which is paradise in the minds of Islamic terrorists. We are fortunate that the Chess match ended as it did. If Bashoul had been taken into custody, in all likelihood he would have languished, at tax-payers expense in prison, where he would have engaged in converting convicted felons into jihadists. Justice definitely prevailed when we 'check-mated' the beast!"

Scott's explanation as to how the jig-saw puzzle came together was fascinating and having compared the investigation that ended a nightmare to a chess match was brilliant. After Tom put the finishing touch to the telling, the group gathered at the table applauded.

By the time Senior Investigator Thomas Weston was called to the podium to accept his commendation, most in the large gathering had consumed several beverages, and they were in a party mood. Tom shook hands with Superintendent Grayson and the other dignitaries, accepted his award and lingered at the microphone. The crowd quieted as Tom spoke. "Dear people and fellow law enforcement officers. I intend to keep my remarks brief, as I know you are eager to celebrate. First, I would ask for a moment of silent prayer for the innocent victims of 9/11, and our comrades mercilessly murdered by Islamic terrorists."

The huge gathering immediately went silent and the silence was broken only by coughs and the stifled sound of some folks crying.

After an appropriate interval, Tom said, "We want the families of all victims of this terrorism nightmare to know that their loved ones did not die in vain and they will never be forgotten." When the applause quieted, he added, "The reign of terror by the man - not really man but demon – who is not worthy of being referred to by name, and who was unquestionably the 20th 9/11 terrorist, is over. I salute all those who devoted themselves in the effort to end the nightmare and want to point out that the 20th terrorist was unwittingly responsible for creating something good. We received wonderful cooperation from members of the Royal Canadian Mounted Police and in the process developed personal bonds of friendship. We owe our friends and fellow professionals from across the border praise and appreciation for their invaluable assistance."

The audience responded by standing, clapping and cheering. When they resumed sitting, Tom continued: "I would like to thank our Commanders for their support in providing the manpower, equipment and funds needed to end the nightmare."

Another round of applause, followed by: "We also owe much thanks, love and appreciation to family members who carried on the functions of running the family, while worrying and praying that the nightmare would end. In that regard I wish to personally commend my devoted and loving wife for enduring the absence of her husband for days on end. Elizabeth, my love, your years of sacrifice are at an end. My 25-years in the 'other' family that I have been devoted to, otherwise known as the New York State Police, is about to end. I will be submitting my retirement tomorrow. That does not mean that I intend to disconnect from my State Police family. Not at all, you all will remain dear to me in retirement and I look forward to a continued relationship.

In conclusion, I invite everyone to join me in singing 'God Bless America.'" He turned, pointed to the band assembled at the back of the room and music began to fill the room.

Without being asked, everyone stood, and the room thundered with the sound of patriotism.

End

ABOUT THE AUTHOR

Wayne E. Beyea retired from a lengthy career in the New York State Police as a trooper and investigator. He earned his criminal justice degree from Ulster County Community College and graduated from the Hostage Negotiation Program at the FBI Academy, Quantico. Author of Fatal Impeachment and more, he is married with five kids and now lives in Atlanta, Georgia.

Printed in the United States
By Bookmasters